I'LL BE BACK

BOBBIE ROBINS

Copyright © 2022 by Bobbie Robins

All rights reserved.

No part of this publication may be reproduced, distributed, or transmitted in any form or by any means, including photocopying, recording, or other electronic or mechanical methods, without the prior written permission of the publisher, except as permitted by U.S. copyright law.

The story, all names, characters, and incidents portrayed in this production are fictitious. No identification with actual persons (living or deceased), places, buildings, and products is intended or should be inferred.

Edited by Kate Seger

Cover by TMT Cover Design

Acknowledgements

I would like to thank my editor, Kate Seger, for the great job, and also my cover creator TMT Cover Design.

CONTENTS

1. Bob Morris   1
2. Ten Hours Ago   13
3. Agent Morris   21
4. The Chase Starts   30
5. Harley's Past   35
6. Boston   42
7. The Old Case   54
8. Revenge   62
9. The Library   73
10. The Yearbook   77
11. The Meeting   81
12. The Old Case: The Students   89
13. Bob   96

14.	Harley	100
15.	The List of Next Victims	109
16.	The Clues from the Diary	115
	Fullpage image	120
17.	The Call	121
18.	Updates	126
19.	At the Restaurant	135
20.	Harley and Alfred	142
21.	At Alfred's Home	152
22.	The FBI and Harley	158
23.	The Rhyme	171
24.	Alfred's Book	176
25.	The Reason	184
26.	Bob and Harley	190
	Also By Bobbie Robins	202
	Also By The Author	203

Chapter 1

BOB MORRIS

One, two, three, four, five,
 Once I caught a girl alive,
Six, seven, eight, nine, ten,
Then I let you go again.
Why did I let you go?
Because you hurt me so.

Agent Bob Morris winced as he turned in his bed and listened to the same rhyme over and over again. His injured shoulder ached, and he'd skipped his physical therapy again. He was obsessed with the rhyme Harley Whitlock had sung during the abductions and the shooting that had injured his shoulder.

He was still on sick leave from the FBI, and he wouldn't be able to return until he passed a physical examination and a psychiatric evaluation. He didn't care. He got up and chugged a glass of water with some painkillers. He drew the curtains. A drab rainy day outside. He shrugged and walked to the kitchen. He started his coffee machine and switched on the television. He turned to the stove but froze when he heard the broadcaster announce the breaking news.

The camera focused on the young female reporter in a TV crew jacket holding a microphone right in front of her. She pushed her long locks of dark hair behind her ear and introduced herself. "This is Meghan Hart from WXCM News, reporting from the scene of the accident."

The camera turned to view the road and the forest behind the reporter. "As you can see, the prison vehicle collided with a deer. The vehicle veered over to the side of the road and rolled over." The camera zoomed to the crash site—a lot of blood and a crushed mess of burned metal. The windshield was cracked and bloody. A deer was stuck in the windshield, the antlers protruding through the broken glass. The rescue crew had pulled out the bodies from the vehicle and covered them with black plastic.

"So far, we have not heard if anyone survived the crash. The fire made it difficult for the rescuers to identify who survived and who didn't. We know the driver and the guard sitting next to him were killed by the deer. When the driver was killed, the vehicle crashed and went off the road."

Bob brushed his fingers through his dark, uncombed hair. The coffee was brewing, and the machine was making a gurgling sound, but Bob didn't pay any attention. He had a sinking feeling in his stomach. He was still frozen in place, staring at the screen.

"I have with me Sheriff Langdon, whose troop arrived at the scene first with the firefighters." The news reporter turned to the somber-looking man in a tan uniform standing next to her. "Do you have more information about who was being transported and how many casualties we have?"

The sheriff cleared his throat and turned his sharp eyes to the camera. "We know now that the transportation crew included four prison guards: the driver, Matt Hammel, and the guard sitting next to him, Paul Calvert, were killed immediately when the deer hit the windshield. They were impaled by its antlers." He paused and frowned. "The two other guards were in the back of the vehicle with the prisoner. He was being transported to the nearby courthouse. His name is Harley Whitlock. Now, at this point, we have found only two bodies, in the back of the vehicle and two in front. The two bodies in the back were both severely burned. We cannot identify them."

When Bob heard the prisoner's name, his legs gave up, and he scrambled to the nearest chair and sat.

"Are you saying you are not sure if the prisoner escaped or if he is one of the deceased?"

"That's correct. Until we identify the bodies at the coroner's office, we can't tell for sure who has died."

Harley is out again? Bob thought. He glanced around the kitchen to locate his cell phone. *Where did I leave it?*

He saw it by the coffee maker, took a few steps, and picked it up. He had turned it off last night. He turned it back on, and the phone started chirping with messages.

He groaned as he saw the list of messages and unanswered calls. His boss had called and left numerous messages. Also, he'd received a call from Samantha a few minutes ago.

She must have heard it on the news like I did, he thought, wincing.

The phone rang, and he answered. "Hello."

"Bob, did you see the news?" his supervisor, Special Agent In charge Michael Walton, asked with a flat voice, not revealing anything.

Bob remembered what he looked like: a lean, tall guy with salt-and-pepper hair. The last time he had seen him had been a week ago when he'd skipped another physical therapy session and his psychiatrist's evaluation; his supervisor had been contacted. Bob had been reprimanded and reminded he wouldn't be able to get back to normal duty until he finished both tasks.

"Yes, I just watched the WXCM news report."

"Harley Whitlock was in that transportation. We have requested the medical examiner to speed up the process of identifying the bodies. We don't know if he survived the crash and is on the run. One of the bodies could be his, but I don't believe so."

"Because why would a guard run away from the scene?" Bob Morris added and sighed. "Yes, I agree. We can safely assume Harley is on the run. But where would he go?"

"That's why I called you. You know him. You've talked to him. And his previous partner, Dr. Talon. I want you on this case."

"But I haven't finished my therapy. And I skipped the psychiatric sessions."

"I know you have, and I have signed a release form. You'll be a consultant on this case. Not on official duty. I think your head is in order, but you'll need PT to get your shoulder back in shape."

"What do you want me to do first?" Bob asked, resigned.

"Whatever you think is best to catch this guy. I remember how difficult it was last time. Bye!"

Bob stared at the phone for a moment and then tapped Samantha's number. She answered immediately.

"Hello, Samantha. This is Bob Morris."

"Is he out again?" she asked in a breathless voice.

"It's possible. We don't know."

"Are you on this case?"

"Sort of. I'm a consultant. Not on official duty due to my gunshot wound."

"Can you inform me when you know for sure if it's him or not?"

"Yes, I can do that." Bob paused and added, "But to be safe, I think you should leave the Albany area with your family, including your mother. Go to the Caribbean or a cabin in Alaska. Go somewhere far away. Don't let anyone at the FBI or anyone else know where you go. Keep this phone with you. I'll keep you updated."

He heard a sigh and a sob. "Okay. Okay, I'll do that."

Samantha had married a few months after her father's funeral and had a baby now. She had married the real Thomas Austin—the one Harley had pretended to be—the owner of the security business. He had dark hair and hazel eyes, just like Harley. That's why Harley had stolen his identity because of the similarities in their facial structure, hair and eye color, and height. But this Thomas was a decent man, not a criminal or a sociopath.

Harley had changed his appearance after the first visit to prison, shaving his head and using dark-framed glasses. Nobody would think of him as Thomas now.

"What does he look like today?" Samantha asked quietly. "I want to know if I have to look out for him."

"I hope you don't." Bob scratched his chin. "The last time I saw him was after the sentencing. His hair had grown. It was down to his ears, a bit curly And his hair was brown, not blond, black, or cut short like he had had before. He had lifted weights and was more muscled than I remembered. But I don't know if that's how he looks today. That was almost a year ago."

"Thank you. I'll leave today," Samantha said. "Goodbye."

"Bye," Bob replied and ended the call. He put the cell phone on the table, went to the coffee machine, and poured a cup of steaming hot coffee. He inhaled. He lifted the cup to his lips and was about to drink when his phone chirped. He glanced at it and frowned.

An unknown number. Then he saw the text message.

—I'm back!—

He dropped the cup on the floor, and it smashed into pieces. He reached out to the table and leaned on it as he re-read the message.

Harley! He's out. He's playing cat and mouse with me!

Bob's face paled to the color of a white sheet as he remembered the shooting incident and how one of his coworkers, Dr. Theresa Talon, the FBI profiler, had turned against them and shot them, including his partner, Jess Ramon. Bob had been shot in the shoulder and recovered but later discovered everyone else had died. His supervisor was right: he had the most knowledge of Whitlock and his past. He had to be involved in capturing him—again!

He called his supervisor, and when he heard his voice, Bob quickly said, "Harley sent me a message. It said: 'I'm back!' The number is unknown."

He heard a deep sigh. "Then it's confirmed. We must start a manhunt. Can you send that message and the number to me? We can try to trace the number."

"Sure, but Harley is not that stupid. It's probably a prepaid or stolen phone, and he has gotten rid of it by now."

"We can still pinpoint where he was when he texted you. And start the chase from there."

"Sure, I'll do it now. And let me know what you find out."

Bob hung up and forwarded the message.

He stepped carefully over the broken pieces of the cup, put on his slippers, took a towel, wiped the floor, and threw the shards of the cup into the trash. He took a new cup from the cupboard, poured some coffee, took out two slices of bread, and made toast. They were ready in a couple of minutes. He cracked a couple of eggs into a frying pan, placed two slices of bacon in another pan and let them sizzle. His moves were automatic; his brain was already processing what he had heard and what he knew about Harley.

After quickly eating his breakfast, he went to his bedroom, took a shower, and got dressed in jeans and a black T-shirt. *Not on official duty*, he reminded himself.

He grabbed a black jacket from the closet on his way out. He wanted to see the scene of the accident before deciding on his next steps. This was bad news for Harley's previous victims. He had promised to go after them and their families when he was sentenced, and now he was out.

Who will his first target be? Bob wondered as he opened his car door, started the engine, and drove toward the crash site.

Chapter 2
Ten Hours Ago

Harley Whitlock sat in the back of the prison transport van and stared at the grim-looking guard in front of him. Another one was sitting at his right side. He wore an orange jumpsuit and was shackled by his feet to the floor and was in handcuffs. Both guards were armed.

The one at his side glanced at his cell phone and texted something. He said to his coworker, "We'll arrive at the exit soon. We'll be at the courthouse in half an hour. No traffic delays."

His partner nodded and gave Harley a quick look. Their prisoner looked relaxed. Nothing seemed to worry him.

Harley hummed something as if he had not a care in the world. The guard next to him frowned. *Why does the prisoner look so carefree and almost happy?*

They all knew he had been sentenced to decades in prison for several crimes, including aggravated assault and kidnapping, killing federal agents, ID theft, and so on. The court didn't even have all the abduction cases when the prosecution started; the prosecutor's office proceeded with what they had instead of waiting for more cases to be proved. Other states fought to get his ass to their courts, but the capital city held its precedence and kept the trial there. Harley's defense attorney had claimed that his client would not get a fair trial in that area because of the infamous Raven abduction. The court rejected this claim and denied the change to another jurisdiction because Harley had committed crimes in several states, so it was said he wouldn't get a fairer trial anywhere else. Harley was sentenced, and his attorney had appealed. Now they were heading to the courthouse to hear another appeal case.

Harley knew that one of these days, he would find out a way to escape, and thus, he continued to let his attorney file appeals and get court dates.

The road in front of them was clear; the driver was casually changing the radio channel, and his coworker was checking his cell phone for messages. Neither one of them was paying attention to the roadside where a herd of deer were eating grass. Some of the deer perked their ears when they heard a car coming, but some just stayed eating. A ten-point buck veered from the group and jumped in front of the approaching vehicle. The driver didn't have time to react when the deer's massive body hit the hood. Its huge black eyes stared at the driver and his partner for a half-second, and then his antlers broke through the window, his hooves hit the passengers, and his antlers impaled the bodies. Only seconds had passed, and the front of the car was a bloody mess.

In the back of the van, the guards and the prisoner didn't know what had happened. They'd felt the impact and the car tossing and turning. Another hard impact made the guards fly against the roof and back to the floor, hitting their backs and heads.

The prisoner was shackled, and his body restrained in his seat, and that saved him from serious injuries. Although his head knocked against the wall, the impact wasn't that severe. He regained consciousness after a few minutes, and he shook his head. He realized the van had crashed, but he didn't know how seriously.

The guard who had been sitting at his side was now stretched on the floor, his neck at a weird angle.

Dead, Harley thought and glanced at the other guard. He was breathing, but he had a large gash on his forehead. *He might be a goner too*, he thought. He pulled him closer with his leg, so he could reach his keys and free himself. He listened, but there were no other sounds from inside the van or outside.

The driver and the other guard must be either unconscious or dead.

When Harley opened his ankle shackles, he got up and stretched his legs and then took a step toward the door. He opened it, listened, and when there were no sounds, he jumped out. Quickly, he checked the situation and saw what had happened. He was alone and alive. He viewed his surroundings: a thick forest on both sides of the road. *No wonder the deer liked it*, he thought. *Lucky for me, though, that I didn't get hurt.*

Great! I have some time to change and get out of this area. The other guard said they're not expecting me at the courthouse for another half an hour.

Harley shook his head. *I bet they didn't test this shatterproof glass with a buck that size!* He chuckled, and he was right.

This vehicle didn't have bulletproof glass, and it wasn't the large transportation van used for transporting several inmates. Harley hadn't been considered a life-threatening prisoner even though he had killed several agents. He wasn't a serial killer, a mafioso, or a leader of a drug cartel.

Harley pulled the unconscious guard out of the van, took off his shoes, undressed him, and switched clothes with him. Then he hopped back inside the van and went to the gun locker in front of the car, opened it, and took out the guns and a shotgun. He smiled. He was ready to go. This area was familiar to him. The van had been heading to the center of the capital city when the crash happened, and he knew that city well. Easier to go in that direction. *Also, I can get lost in a big city*, he thought. *If any vehicles come by, they will see a guard and not a dangerous criminal.*

The uniform had some blood on it, but otherwise, it was his size. Harley brushed his brown hair behind his ears. It had grown longer in prison.

They know what I look like. I need to make some changes. Perhaps I'll cut my hair into a different style. I cannot go bald again. New frames or sunglasses would alter my appearance too, he thought.

However, no cars came by until the next crossroads, and when he got there, he saw a gas station near the corner. He waited for one driver to go inside, then Harley entered his vehicle, a used black truck with some rust on the bottom. Harley made sure no one was watching as he looked for the keys; he was lucky—the owner had left them in the ignition. Quietly, he started the car. A big smile brightened his face when he heard the engine start to purr. He sped away before anyone alerted the owner inside the station.

It was rainy, and mist covered the windshield. He turned on the windshield wipers and the radio, tuning into the news channel—just traffic news, weather, and daily politics.

Nothing yet about the crash, he observed changing channels. *No news is good news*, he thought. *With a full tank of gas, I'll have time to go far, far away if I want.*

I must change my appearance before starting anything else.

Free! Harley thought and smiled. *What should I do next?*

Chapter 3

Agent Morris

The misty rain had stopped, but clouds covered the gray sky.

Agent Bob Morris drove to the scene of the accident. He wanted to find out as much as he could about what had happened with the prison transport. His supervisor, SAC Michael Walton, stood there in his gray suit and tie. When he saw Bob Morris climb out of his car, he waved him closer.

Morris nodded and viewed the scene while approaching his supervisor.

"One of the guards was not wearing a uniform. The first responders thought he was the prisoner, but after we confirmed his identity by taking his fingerprints, we now know for sure. Harley Whitlock has taken his uniform and is on the run."

Bob Morris kept glancing at the scene. It looked like a deer accident. It had hit the front windshield with force, and the driver and the guard next to him had died on impact. No problem there. But the prisoner must have been secured with chains so he wouldn't have hurt himself in the impact as he couldn't move. Thus, the guard in the back of the van must have been the one that was injured; a sudden stop would have caused his body to fly forward, possibly causing him to hit his head and neck. No wonder he was unconscious. Three covered bodies were next to the van. The medical examiner was about to transport them away. *Fine, let him do that*, Bob thought. *There is nothing suspicious about the accident. Harley just got lucky.*

Bob glanced ahead and then turned around, assessing where Harley could have run.

Not into the forest. Bob squinted. His eyes roamed the accident site. Dense and impenetrable forest covered the roadsides. This was not yet the capital city where the trees were cut and trimmed, and the lush green grass was cut every week. This was still an uninhabited road—nobody wanted to live close to the prison.

He turned to view the intended direction of the van. *Albany. That's where Samantha lives. That's the area Harley knows well. That's where he went. But what is his plan? Does he have a plan?*

Bob's supervisor asked, "What do you think?"

"He went that way, to Albany. He knows it well. He probably has a hiding place there and cash to use. I'm sure we didn't get all his funds when we arrested him and froze his known accounts. He had used several aliases. He knows computers and technology and how to hide and transfer money without leaving a trail. It was just bad luck that he hadn't known about Talon's diary. Without it, we would have never caught him." Bob brushed his fingers through his hair, making it stick up. He shook his head. "How are we going to find him this time? We don't have a diary to follow.

We don't have a trail?" He said this more to himself than to his boss.

"We'll catch him. We always do." SAC Walton patted him on the back and walked to his car. "Where do you plan to start?"

"The usual routine. Check for stolen vehicles. Check local gas stations and their cameras. Any convenience stores nearby with working cameras," Bob replied. "He has a prison guard's uniform, so he should be identifiable in the images if he got caught on any cameras."

"Keep me updated. I want to know about any leads and any ideas you get. You're a consultant, not officially an agent."

"Yes, I know." Bob waved and walked back to his car, back to chasing the shrewdest criminal he had ever met.

***

While driving along the road leading to Albany, the same route Harley had taken, Bob kept an eye out for nearby buildings.

The rain started again, and the drops pattered against the windshield. He drove to the next crossroad with a gas station, and he saw a local police car parked in front of it.

This might be my lucky day. Bob slowed and turned to park behind the police vehicle. He went inside, where the police officer was interviewing the clerk and the customer, who looked agitated. Bob caught him saying, "And my truck is gone! Stolen!"

"Excuse me," Bob interrupted. "I'm Bob Morris from the FBI. I need to look at your CCTV footage." He pointed at the cameras. "Are they working?"

"Yes, they are. If you come through to the back, I can show you," the clerk said. He was a young man with a checkered shirt and jeans. Eager to please, he came out from behind the desk, but the customer stopped them.

He grabbed Bob's arm and demanded, "What about my truck?"

Bob glanced down at the man's hand, and the customer, an angry middle-aged man with a potbelly, dirty jeans, and a too-tight T-shirt, released his arm and asked again, "What about my truck?"

Bob nodded to the police officer, a young man with a crew cut, and said, "He will take all your information, and then we'll let you know if and when we find your truck."

The customer shook his head, turned back to the officer, and continued giving his contact information, his truck details, and his license plate. "How am I going to get back to work from here?" He shook his head once more and gestured outside. "This is in the middle of nowhere!"

"I can drive you where you need to go," the officer offered. "Just give me a minute. I will talk to the FBI agent first." He walked to the backroom where the clerk had taken Bob.

"Excuse me." The young police officer knocked on the doorframe and interrupted Bob and the gas station clerk. "I have the information about the stolen truck. Do you need it?"

"Yes, please, thank you." Bob took out his phone and walked to the police officer, who handed over his notepad. Bob took a photograph of the page where he had written all the information.

"I hope you can read my notes." The police officer chuckled. "My handwriting is not that good."

"I'm sure I can. And if I can't, I'll contact you. I need your name and phone number," Bob replied and added, "My number is on the card." He handed him his business card.

"Sure. Let me text you that." The police officer took out his cell phone and glanced at the card, entering Bob's number. After a second, Bob's phone chimed.

"Thanks." Bob nodded.

"I'll take the owner of the stolen vehicle back home," the officer replied, gesturing toward the waiting customer.

"Great. He needs a ride, and you can question him on the way back. See if he remembers anything else or if he saw anyone hanging around," Bob commented.

The officer hesitated by the doorway and asked, "Is this stolen vehicle related to a federal case?"

"It might be. I'm checking now if the person who took it is someone I know," Bob replied and turned back to the camera.

The clerk had rewound the footage to the timeframe when the truck had been stolen. Bob leaned in closer. A man in a guard's uniform had come from the direction of the accident. He glanced around, checked the parked cars. One of them was the clerk's car, and the other one was probably another customer inside the store and then he saw him opening the truck's door. The owner must have left the keys inside because it was so easy for Harley to start the vehicle and drive away.

"That's him," Bob muttered and pointed at the camera.

It was weird to see Harley out again. He looked different from the last time. He had long hair almost reaching his shoulders, and he stroked it while sneaking around and checking the parked vehicles. Bob turned to the police officer and commented, "Yes, the one who stole that man's truck is the prisoner that escaped this morning. He's now wanted by the FBI. He has killed several people before. The truck will be confiscated when we find it. You can let the owner know that. He won't get it back for a while. But it might also be destroyed. I don't think this escaped prisoner will want to leave a trail."

The police officer nodded and left.

Bob turned back to the footage. Harley had taken the road to Albany.

He texted that to his boss and then took a photo of the footage of Harley wearing the guard's bloody uniform and facing the camera and sent that to him too.

Chapter 4

THE CHASE STARTS

Bob Morris viewed the roads leading away from the gas station. He knew, based on the video, that the fugitive had headed toward the center of Albany. And he had been gone for hours now. Would it be possible to follow him?

He scratched his chin and squinted. Last time it had been almost impossible to find him.

He could ask the FBI to check out the traffic cameras, the ATM cameras, and the shops on this road, but what then? It would take hours, if not days, to follow that route.

His phone chirped with a new text message. He pulled it out and checked who had texted. It was Michael Walton.

—Thanks for the update. We'll keep an eye on the truck. Nothing new on this end. Keep me posted. Mike.—

Yeah, I knew that, Bob thought and put his phone back in his pocket. *How would you have anything new yet because you are there, and I'm following the trail of this killer?*

Bob sat inside his car, and before starting it, he just leaned back. *What would I do in Harley's situation? I would ditch that truck or burn it, find new clothes, and go to my stash of cash or wherever I hid some money in case I ever got out.* His eyes darkened. *If I were Harley, I would also find the one woman who got away: Samantha!*

He picked up his phone and called Samantha. It went to voice mail. "Samantha, this is Bob Morris. I hope you're out of the country by now. Harley is heading toward Albany. Call me if you need updates."

Then he called Samantha's mother, Cynthia Raven, the widow of Carl Raven; Harley had sent the angel of death to his hospital bed. Bob wanted to warn Cynthia that she could be in danger if Harley were after the Raven family.

Cynthia answered almost immediately. "Hello?"

"Cynthia, this is Bob Morris." Bob tried not to sound too worried on the phone. He didn't want Cynthia to overreact.

"Is this about Harley's escape? Samantha called. She is at the airport leaving town. She didn't want to stay in town when she heard that Harley had escaped."

"Oh, good." Bob sounded relieved. "I left her a message and asked her to do that. You should leave too. Harley is heading to the center of Albany. If he goes after Samantha, he might come to look for her at your house."

"I have already packed, and my car is waiting outside. I'll be gone as soon as we finish this call. I'm not going to wait for him to destroy more lives." Cynthia's voice was both angry and scared.

"I'll keep you posted. Bye, now." Bob hung up and then tapped his fingers on the steering wheel.

Where could Harley go? How would he change his appearance this time? He had altered his hair color and eye color in the past. It had been hard to put out any BOLO images of him because no one knew what he looked like. They could make a collage of his previous faces and hairstyles. Perhaps, someone would recognize him.

A few raindrops pattered again on the windshield. Bob started the car and put on the windshield wipers. *What gloomy weather*, he thought as he headed downtown.

While driving, he kept an eye on the roadside. More buildings, some residential and some business buildings, but nothing looked suspicious. No burned truck or smoke anywhere. No abandoned cars or killed drivers along the side of the road. Harley had not stopped here. He had continued his escape and was probably now entering the city limits.

Bob shook his head in frustration as he decided his time was best used if he went back home and waited for updates or tried to get into Harley's mind and figure out where he might be headed next. Bob drove slowly back to his apartment and parked outside the building.

Inside, he tossed his keys on the kitchen table and hung his coat on the back of the chair. He and picked up a new cup for his coffee as he had dropped the previous one. He collected a few porcelain pieces of the cup from the floor and wiped the floor again while the new coffee was brewing.

He strolled to his study and picked up the notes from Harley's previous case.

Bob had copied the diary of Dr. Theresa Talon. She was the FBI profiler who had conspired with Harley.

He looked determined as he grabbed his copies, his handwritten notes, and his tape recorder and took them with him to the kitchen and started combing through them. He hoped he could find something useful.

Chapter 5
Harley's Past

Bob Morris listened to the tapes, but nothing was interesting except that song Harley kept singing to himself. He had recorded it, and he played it again. It sounded like a nursery rhyme, but he had changed the words.

One, two, three, four, five,
Once I caught a girl alive,
Six, seven, eight, nine, ten,
Then I let you go again.
Why did I let you go?
Because I loved you so.

At first, nothing was interesting in Talon's notes. Some meetings with Harley, she had recorded on a tape, but when Bob listened to them, there was nothing unusual. Harley answered just like any other patient would in a psychologist's office. No strange comments or remarks or hints of their partnership or any other relationship. But they had been partners in crime. How come there was nothing about that? Bob frowned and kept on listening. Nothing in the tapes. He sighed and put them aside. He might have to listen to them again sometime, but he decided to move on to the handwritten notes. First, it seemed she had handwritten the conversations with Harley and highlighted some notes with side remarks. But when Bob looked at the side remarks, sometimes she had drawn a line on the side of a chapter and sometimes made an exclamation mark on the side of the paper. Why was that?

One marked paragraph was about Harley's parents and how "they had died in a fire, a suspected arson." Dr. Teresa Talon, his partner, had marked that chapter. Then he read forward, and again she had marked a comment about Harley's parents: *An ordinary couple*. And the next one said, *An ordinary family. Nothing there*. There was a big exclamation mark next to that line.

Is Dr. Talon telling me to check on Harley's family and his parents? Bob scratched his chin. It seemed like there was something she wanted the reader to note about Harley's family.

Bob had browsed through his notes when he visited Samantha's parents after Harley had been released from prison. What was it Dr. Talon had said about Harley's parents—?

He dug out his notes. Dr. Talon had described Harley as a narcissist and stated that he was extremely interested in issues of personal adequacy and power. Then Dr. Talon said that Harley had worked in mediocre, low-level positions in different places and in different states for the past ten years, which was also quite typical of sociopaths. Dr. Talon had said that these types of personality disorders are difficult because these people aren't able to keep their jobs because they consider themselves to be better than others.

But so far, he'd found nothing specific about Harley's parents.

Dr. Talon had said that Harley wanted revenge and to cause trouble for Samantha's family. Bob almost chuckled. *Trouble, yeah!* He sent his accomplice to kill Carl Raven when Samantha's father was in the hospital recovering from a heart attack.

The next comments were also obvious: *Harley will take on another identity because he can't use the names he has used before. And he will try to change his name and his appearance.*

But Dr. Talon had not mentioned anything about his parents specifically. Why had she marked those paragraphs in her interviews then?

Bob browsed through the case file that the FBI had compiled on Harley. He started reading the file he had read many times before.

The FBI's file had been compiled based on Harley's public records. And that only told them that he'd had a normal life until his parents died in a fire when he was seventeen. Arson was suspected, but no one was arrested. Harley was questioned, but the investigators could not prove that he had anything to do with the fire that killed his parents.

Bob closed his notes and frowned. If there was something there, he didn't see it.

He went to the kitchen to make another cup of coffee and made a cheese and ham sandwich. He ate, leaning against the kitchen counter.

It was not because he was in a hurry, but his mind churned the facts he had read.

Then he rushed back to the notes and browsed the papers again, looking for a birth certificate. There had to be a birth certificate somewhere. He couldn't find it. He went online and searched for it. He found only a note which stated Harley's birth date as November 20, 1989. His mother's name was listed as Charlotte Meghan Keller.

Bob realized what was wrong. All the notes talked about his parents, but the birth information only mentioned his mother. He looked through the public records to find out when Charlotte Meghan Keller married. Her marriage was dated November 11, 1992. Three years after Harley was born!

That's what Dr. Talon wanted me to notice in her notes.

She had realized the same thing: Harley's father was not his biological father.

Who was Harley's father? Was there something Dr. Talon had found out and wanted the next investigators to know too?

I have to find out. Bob picked up his cell phone and called his boss. When he answered, he said, "Bob here. I need to take a trip to Boston and find out more about Harley's first years. His father is not mentioned in the birth records, and we don't know who his birth father is. His mother married three years after Harley was born."

He listened to his supervisor for a moment and then replied, "I don't know if that lead will go anywhere. I have a feeling that Dr. Talon had marked the notes for the next investigator. She knew Harley's personality and what he could do to the people around him. I don't think she ever truly trusted Harley. And that turned out to be a right concern as Harley killed her. About the notes, Dr. Talon only marked the paragraphs mentioning Harley's parents. She might have found out something that will help us in this case."

His supervisor said something, and Bob replied, "Yes, I will keep you posted. Bye, now."

And it was time to check out the flights to Boston.

Chapter 6

BOSTON

———◆◯◆———

Bob landed at Boston Airport the following morning, headed to a rental car office, and signed out an inconspicuous sedan. As he was a consultant and not an official FBI agent, he was more restricted in his skills, ideas, and available resources, than a normal agent would be, but he preferred it like it was now because it gave him the freedom to pursue his ideas and follow his instincts, and he didn't have to sign off every single car and gun he used. He didn't have a gun with him. It would have been too much hassle to get it through security at the airport, so he traveled light: just the clothes he had on and a small leather shoulder bag that contained some notes, pens, his cell phone, and charger.

The sky was cerulean blue with some white clouds. *It's a nice day for a day trip*, he thought as he headed to the hospital of St. Mary's, where Harley was born.

St. Mary's was an old hospital but still used for emergencies and urgent care. When Bob walked in and asked about old patient documents, the front desk clerk said, "All the documents are stored in the basement. If you are not a relative, you won't be able to access any documents in the archives."

Bob nodded and replied, "I work for the FBI.

"Then you know you need a warrant to access any old birth certificates."

That didn't help him. Not that he needed to get a warrant. The hospital was his first stop. If he decided he needed a warrant, he could ask his boss to send one.

Next, Bob headed to the library. It wasn't far away from the hospital, and it took him only ten minutes to drive there.

When he parked outside in the parking lot, he viewed the building. He locked his car and strolled to the front door. The heavy wooden door creaked when he pulled it open. The entrance hallway was as old-fashioned as the exterior, with a waist-high formal desk at the far end with a clerk and a computer to help if you needed any. The library's entrance hall was spacious, and you could see to the back behind the clerk's desk where all the dozens of bookshelves and cataloged items were located.

Bob followed the instructions on the shelves and picked out a stack of newspapers and took them to a reading table. He placed the stack in front of him and sat down.

He preferred to browse real newspapers instead of using the computer and browsing the archives, which had more items.

In the newspaper archive, you would have to know what you were looking for, and Bob didn't know yet what he was looking for and what he hoped to find. He browsed through old newspapers of the time

Harley was born. And there he hit the jackpot. March 1989 had front-page news of a rape.

He took photos of the newspaper article and went to look for other ones from the same week. More news on the same topic: Rape. A local college girl was raped. A suspected college hazing went wrong. A twenty-year-old student, Charlotte Meghan Keller was the victim. Harley's mother! Bob did some quick calculations. If Harley was born on November 20, 1989, then he was a child of this rape. And who could be his real father? He browsed the news and found out that the fraternity of the αβΩ was suspected of gang rape. But as the victim had been drinking and could not identify her attackers, the charges were dropped.

Bob sent the images of the news of March 1989 to his boss, who texted back.

—Great work!—

Bob smiled wryly. *Great work if it leads somewhere. Now, time to go to the police station and find out more.*

As he drove the short distance to the police station, he considered his choices. He could introduce himself as an FBI agent and let them contact his boss, or he could tell them he was a consultant working with the feds to find out more about the fugitive. He parked outside a gray building and walked up the stairs. The station door required a hefty push, and it opened with a groan.

As Bob walked in, he glanced around the large waiting room. Chairs were arranged against white walls covered by photographs of missing persons and notices about how to protect homes from unwanted intruders. He noticed an information desk with an elderly gray-haired police officer behind it. The man gave him a look with wary eyes as he stopped in front of his desk. "What can we do for you, sir?"

"I hope you can help me find out more about a decades-old rape case," Bob said. "I'm a consultant working for the FBI."

"It's better if you go through that door and find Sergeant Garrison. He can help you." He buzzed the door open and let Bob walk in. The bullpen was busy with officers walking and talking, drinking coffee, or exchanging notes. No handcuffed criminals anywhere. This was the detectives' side of the police department, he concluded as he slowly sauntered to find out where he could find Sergeant Garrison.

He saw a glass door on his left with the name *Sgt. Garrison*. *That's the one*, he thought and knocked on the door.

"Come in!"

He heard a gruff voice from inside; he opened the door and saw a man in his fifties sitting behind a desk full of papers and files. The sergeant glanced up and saw Bob standing in the doorway.

"Who are you, and what do you want?" Sergeant Garrison said tiredly. He didn't have time for investigations related to ancient cases. His front desk had informed him about this man.

"My name is Bob Morris, and I'm a consultant working with the FBI, and we are chasing a fugitive."

Garrison took off his glasses and rubbed his nose; his glasses had left a red mark on both sides of his face.

"We don't hear that very often. Care to share what case it is you're looking for?"

"In March 1989, a young student was raped. Her name was Charlotte Meghan Keller."

Garrison froze. He stared at Bob for a long time and then sighed. "I know that case. I was a rookie when it happened. It was bad. A gang rape. Multiple suspects. Rich kids from the college with famous attorneys on their side. Dads with deep pockets." Garrison shook his head. "We had plenty of evidence: fibers, partial fingerprints, DNA samples from her clothes and under her nails. But what sank the case was the college counselor. They had asked Charlotte to sign a statement before she went to the hospital, and they reported the gang rape to us. She had said she was drunk and didn't remember much of anything of that evening. She had woken up half-naked, her skirt up round her waist with no underpants. She had semen stains on her legs. The counselors had told her to go clean up and take a shower before going to the hospital."

Bob frowned. "She shouldn't have done that or signed any statement before talking with you guys."

"Yeah, I know. But she did. And after that, the expensive suits denied us interviews with their clients because the victim had destroyed evidence and signed a statement in which she clearly stated she did not remember anything. How could she know if it was consensual sex or not?"

Bob shook his head. "She was intimidated into signing. And someone knew it was a gang rape and was protecting their offspring from getting a criminal record and being sentenced. A kid's future would be damaged if he had a rape conviction. But they never considered that they destroyed the victim's life and future. Did they even know she had a rapist's child?"

"I don't know if they ever checked that out. I didn't know she had a child." Garrison leaned back in his chair, and it creaked under his weight. "I was still excited to be a young detective, and that case left a bad taste in my mouth. You're welcome to check up on that one, and you can have my handwritten personal notes too." He called the archives and told them to dig out the file. Then he reached out to his desk drawer and pulled out a worn notebook. "My notes." He handed it to Bob. "I always kept it close in case something new came up and we could do her justice."

Bob got up and said, "I hope so. And we still have her son to catch. I'm still not sure how this old case is connected to his crimes, but I have a hunch it is."

He turned to walk away but then stopped and asked, "Did you ever hear a song or a rhyme which goes like this—" He took out his tape recorder and played back Harley's little song.

One, two, three, four, five,
Once I caught a girl alive,
Six, seven, eight, nine, ten,
Then I let you go again.
Why did I let you go?
Because you hurt me so.

Garrison frowned. "Replay that to me."

Bob played it again and watched as Garrison jotted down some quick notes on the notepad in front of him. He waited until Garrison had finished and said, "You figured out something."

"Maybe, yeah. Ten rapists who hurt her and let her go."

"Good one. That could be the answer." Bob took out his notes and wrote that down.

"And she had a page of a nursery rhyme book with her when we talked to her in the hospital. We thought she had ripped it in the place where she was raped. Now that sounds even more believable," Garrison added.

"What was the page about?" Bob turned his gaze to the sergeant.

"About catching fishes. Like the one you played." Bob nodded. If the victim didn't rip the page off then there was also another choice: someone else gave her the page, but Bob had no idea why.

"Interesting. Do you know the book it had been taken from?"

Garrison shook his head. "No, we got nowhere with that page. It was just a page from an old book. We couldn't even identify the writer of the poem. We checked with the library, and they said the writer was unknown, but they could trace versions of it back to the 1800s."

"Not much of a clue then." Bob snapped his notebook closed and said, "I'll visit the archives now. Have a good day."

"Keep me posted. I want to know what you find out in your investigation!" Garrison shouted after him.

Bob waved in acknowledgment and then headed to the archives. He had to ask for directions once, but eventually, he found his way to the basement, and there he saw a narrow desk with an officer waiting for him.

"Sign here, please." The officer handed him a paper to release the evidence.

Bob signed and grabbed the evidence box. He glanced around and then turned back and asked, "Where can I go and view this box? I don't want to take it with me to a hotel."

"If you go around the corner, you'll find a desk and chairs. It's a small room, but it has a good light to read," the officer replied, pointing to the direction where he would find that room.

The case box was old, moldy, and dusty smelling. It had a handwritten note on the side which stated the case number, the victim's name, the date of the incident.

He pulled out a chair, sat down, and opened the box.

Down the rabbit hole, he thought.

Chapter 7
THE OLD CASE

The old case box held a plastic bag that contained torn and stained clothes. Bob opened the bag and examined the clothes more thoroughly: a black mini skirt, a pink short-sleeved shirt, torn white bra—cut with a knife from the midsection, he noted—and no underpants. Next, there were white—now dirty—sneakers with some stains on them. *Did they test the stains back then? What are these stains? Some of them look like dirt stains, but some are blood. If they are blood stains, then perhaps some of our perps had a cut? Our laboratory could do more tests if needed,* he considered and wrote a note about that. He thought he should let his boss know so he could decide if the clothes and the sneakers should be retested.

Bob sniffed the clothes. He could still detect the faint smell of cigarettes and perfume.

Did they check on DNA back then? he wondered. *If not, then perhaps we could try to do that now. The science of DNA is more advanced nowadays, and we don't need a big sample, and they can find DNA in clothes even if back then they didn't try to find it.*

He pulled out the case file and placed it on the table. He decided he would read that last.

He took out the yellowed and torn page from a plastic bag and viewed it. It was just as Sergeant Garrison had said: A rhyme about a fish being caught and then released back into the water. The paper looked as if it had been torn from a book, just like he had been told. *No rhyme on the back side of the paper.* It was blank. Bob frowned.

Strange, usually books have either pictures or text on both sides of the page. This must have been the last page of a nursery rhyme book, Bob thought and made a note of that in his notebook.

He took a picture and sent it to his boss, adding a comment.

—This might be something. Harley's mother had it after the rape.—

The phone chirped with a reply almost immediately.

—Good. Keep digging. I'll circulate it to see if anyone can identify it.—

—No one here at Boston Library could. And one more thing: it might be the last page of a nursery rhyme book. There are no images or texts on the back of the rhyme. The empty page is usually at the end of a book. If it were from the front, then the back side would have an image of the next poem or something else.—

—Okay. I'll inform the investigators. Anything else?—

—Yes. The sergeant here recognized the rhyme that Harley sang. He said the numbers could refer to the number of rapists involved in her mother's case. I agree. It fits.—

Bob noted that his boss must have got tired of texting as he noticed his phone buzz.

Bob answered. "Yes."

"Okay. So, should we start looking at that old case now?" Michal Walton asked. His voice was sharp.

Bob hesitated. "I'm going through that case file right now. It won't help much if there are no clues about who the rapists were. However, I have a hunch that all of Whitlock's crimes are linked to this old case. His humming of that rhyme while he is killing or extorting people. I got a feeling that he's on a revenge path."

"He wants to avenge his mother's rape. Makes sense. More than our theory of random killings. Perhaps you were right: Talon left you a clue when she had marked comments on her notes of Harley," Michael replied.

"Also, you should consider asking for this case file and retesting the clothes and the sneakers for DNA.

Some stains are dirt, but some are blood. We don't know if all the stains are from Harley's mother."

"Okay, I will do that. Anything else?"

"No, not at the moment. I just started here," Bob replied.

"Keep digging. We'll follow up on any sightings of Harley's sightings here," Michael replied.

"Have you found where he went after the gas station?" Bob asked curiously.

"No. Nothing. He must have torched or hid the van he stole and changed his appearance. We've got no clues to follow." Michael's voice was tired.

"We'll catch him. He will make a mistake," Bob assured. He hoped so. Harley was too dangerous to be free.

"Have you heard from Samantha and her family?" Michael asked and his voice was concerned.

"She left Albany with her family, and her mother was leaving when I called her. I have not heard where they went, and if they reached their destination. I only know their plans to leave," Bob replied. "Should I try to call them?"

"No, better not. Harley could be monitoring their phones and calls. It's better to stay away from them," Michael replied.

"Do you think he has bugged their phones?" Bob asked frowning. He didn't know Samantha's destination or her mother's, but if their phones were bugged, then Harley might have listened to Samantha's calls to her mother and found out. He might be on his way to find them.

"He was a real pro in hacking." Michael sighed in frustration. "I don't know if it's better to leave them alone or contact and make sure they are okay."

"Okay. Let me get back to you if I find anything else here in this evidence box," Bob said tapping the tabletop with his fingers. He was impatient and wanted to start to read the case file. It might have something important.

"Sure. Thanks," Michael said and hang up.

Bob sighed and brushed his hair with his fingers. He had to consider warning the Raven family. He could text both Samantha and her mother and tell them not to reveal their locations. Only, Harley could find out where the messages came from if he had already bugged their phones. *It wouldn't matter if Harley knows where I am*, he thought and quickly texted a message to both women.

—Be aware. Harley might have bugged your phones. Don't reveal your location during phone conversations. If you have done so, then leave and go somewhere else. Bob.—

Samantha was the one Harley had kidnapped several times, and he'd killed her father. It was likely he would want to go after her again. *If he can find her*, Bob thought, frowning.

He didn't expect to get a message back from Samantha, but when his phone chirped and he viewed it, it was a new message from her.

—We're safe. We've not told anyone on the phone or on the computer where we went.—

Good, Bob thought, smiling. *Smart girl*.

Chapter 8

REVENGE

Revenge. Perhaps, Bob thought as he read the nursery rhyme again.

Harley's mother could have gotten the page from a library book or from a home that had a library. An old family home with a nursery and nannies. A home with lots of money. Rich kids of families who had the money to hire attorneys to defend themselves even before the rape case was built, Bob thought as he wrote notes.

Bob didn't find anything useful in Charlotte's clothes when he examined them, but he still wanted the FBI laboratory to recheck them. It made sense to do it again because the science was better now. The local police department had processed the clothes, but all the techniques of finding and processing fibers, hairs, and other stuff had progressed since 1989 when the rapes occurred.

He sighed and rubbed his face with his hands. *Wake up! Get your mojo going!*

He hadn't gotten much sleep lately with his wound aching.

A cup of coffee would be great at this point, he thought, and got up and went to ask the clerk if there was a coffee machine anywhere near. He didn't want to leave the case files alone for too long.

The clerk pointed around the corner. There was a coffee brewing. Not too old, but fresh! *Excellent!* Bob took a paper cup, filled it, and returned to the case file.

He went back to read the notes of the police officers. The descriptions of the suspects were not very long in this case, he observed.

A twenty-year-old student, Charlotte Meghan Keller, was the victim of suspected rape. The fraternity of the αβΩ was the place where she had visited that evening with her roommate Lara Lindell. They had not been drinking before entering the fraternity building where the party was, but inside, they were offered several drinks. Charlotte remembers drinking one of the offered drinks, but not more than that.

Bob paused. She wasn't drunk. Someone could have drugged her.

He continued reading.

Charlotte didn't find her friend Lara when she wanted to leave. She wasn't feeling well.

One of the fraternity boys had shown her a room upstairs where she could rest.

Who was that? Bob wondered. Charlotte had not described him.

Charlotte remembers waking up later that evening. She didn't know how much time had passed. She felt dizzy. And at first, she kept her eyes closed, but then she felt a heavy weight and pain between her legs. She opened her eyes and saw that a guy with a black mask was on top of her, penetrating her. That was probably what woke her up. Her skirt was up to her waist, her pink blouse was pulled up, and her bra was cut open down the middle. She tried to get up, but she couldn't because someone was sitting behind her head, holding her hands above her head so she couldn't move.

She tried to pull her hands out of the tight grip, but the guy behind her laughed and said, "She's enjoying this, aren't you, honey?" and the other boys in the room laughed.

She noted there were eight male students in the room, all with masks. Charlotte recalls saying, "Let me go! Why are you doing this?" whilst turning her head to see the other guys in the room.

Charlotte remembers that someone replied, "This is our initiation ceremony to the frat house. You were chosen to assist us tonight," while the others laughed menacingly.

Charlotte says she felt her heart skip a beat. That she knew she was going to be gang raped. She panicked and cried, but the fraternity buddies seemed to get more excited about that. She stared at her rapists to spot clues about who they were, but they were hard to recognize because of the masks. Some were taller, some skinnier, some sturdier, and some had blond hair, some long dark hair, and some reddish hair.

Charlotte recalls wriggling and begging them to stop, but that the boys had laughed "as if she was just a piece of meat." She'd tried to scream for help, but no one came. She heard distant music, which was probably from downstairs where she had been. Terrified, Charlotte thought that no one would hear her voice over the loud music.

And when one had finished raping her, the next one took his position. Some bit her breasts, some used their fingers inside her before penetrating her, and some just climbed on top of her and pushed hard, seeming to enjoy her screams. The last one was the one who had been behind her holding her arms up above. He let go and quickly climbed on top of her.

Charlotte had already passed out after his friends, so there wasn't any resistance. She recalls opening her eyes when she felt him and trying to push him away but with no luck. She believes she scraped his chin with her nails leaving red marks.

Bob thought that was good. Perhaps there would be some DNA on file collected from under her nails.

When they had done what they had planned to do, they carried her limp body outside the fraternity of the αβΩ building and placed it on the ground next to a tree and left. She was half awake when they did that. She had gotten up and pulled her torn clothes back on to cover her naked and violated body. After seeing the counselor, she returned to her dorm room and took a shower.

A big mistake, Bob thought. *She should have gone to the hospital immediately and then reported the rapes.*

Charlotte changed her clothes, and when she reported the rape to the university nurse, she felt that the university didn't want to believe that anything like that could have happened on their premises and certainly not at the fraternity of the αβΩ building.

Of course not because they wanted to protect their reputation and all the boys in their precious club, Bob thought, frowning. He continued reading.

Charlotte went to the hospital to be checked, and the hospital reported the gang rape to the police. Local police collected some DNA and fibers from her body and from her clothes which they had gotten from her dorm room.

We better still check them, Bob thought.

As he continued to read, Bob learned that when Sergeant Garrison had tried to go to interview the fraternity boys, he had faced a brick wall of expensive suits representing the residents of the fraternity building. They had told him that he was wasting his time. If the girl was drunk and had been raped when she was unconscious and had taken a shower before reporting the rape to the officials, then all the evidence was compromised. It would just be the word of a drunken girl against that of the respectable offspring of several wealthy families. He was asked which one he thought the jury and the judge would believe.

Because of the attorneys, Garrison had decided to look into the case on his own time. Because of his diligence, there was more to find out. When Bob opened his notes of the case, he saw descriptions of the rapists as Charlotte had described: heights, hair color, eye color, and any other clues she could remember.

She had been thorough in paying attention to these rapists, Bob realized.

Her observations were good enough to identify and find some of these boys. For example, a red-haired, short, stocky guy with a hitching voice. There couldn't have been many of those in the class of 1989. Or the one who had green eyes and long black curls. Or the one who had one index finger missing?

All the clues were there, but the attorneys had contacted the prosecutor's office and probably promised a hefty donation to his campaign to be the next Attorney General, or so Bob imagined it had happened because the prosecutor's office had vehemently denied taking this case based on circumstantial evidence and hearsay by a drunken girl.

Harley must have learned about the gang rape when he was a teenager. Bob guessed Harley had planned to find out who his father was.

But why did he burn his home with his mother and stepfather inside? Was his mother the reason he did that? Perhaps Harley had gotten angry because his mother had never told him about what had happened and that he was the result of gang rape, and she couldn't know who his father was. Did Harley want to punish his mother? Or did Harley want to punish his stepfather for pretending to be his father?

Bob sighed, brushed his hand through his hair, and sipped his coffee.

Why so many abductions of young women? How were they connected to Harley's past? Or was everything connected? What if—?

Bob lowered the case file to the tabletop and leaned back. He had a crazy idea.

What if Harley had figured out who the rapists were? All Harley needed was the yearbook of 1989 and to check out the guys who belonged to the

$\alpha\beta\Omega$ fraternity during that school year. He must have found the descriptions of the rapists either from the police records or got them from his mother. Bob leaned toward the latter or both. Matching the descriptions of the rapists to the yearbook wouldn't have been too difficult, especially considering Harley's skills in hacking. He could have hacked the university's database and checked for other similar cases and who had been the guilty ones.

Bob flipped through the case file and pulled out the list of attorneys. *A list of the most wealthy and successful companies on the East Coast*, he thought. They wouldn't give any confidential information freely, not even to the FBI. They would say every conversation with a client was privileged between him and his attorney. Harley could have gone through the back door and hacked his way to their computers and found out the names of those they represented.

Bob took pictures of the list of attorneys' names and sent it to his boss. And the descriptions of the rapists.

There must be something in this case that started Harley's crime spree, he thought.

Bob's phone rang. It was his boss calling back. "These names are the attorneys of the very rich. They are almost untouchable. Don't tell me you plan to go after them?"

Bob chuckled. "No, but I thought we could do a simple internet search and find out the names of the families they usually represent because the attorneys had been at the university the next morning. No delays. They must have been on a retainer."

"Good idea. We can do that. Anything else?"

"Yes, the other list I sent you was descriptions of the rapists in her case. Perhaps we can link the descriptions to some of the families."

"Okay, we can try that. Are you staying long in Boston?"

"No, I think I'll try to find the 1989 yearbook at the university, and then I'll come back," Bob replied.

"Great! See you when you're back," his boss said and ended the call.

Chapter 9

The Library

Bob drove to the university parking lot. The sun had gone behind clouds, but otherwise, the day was nice and warm, and some students were sitting outside, some were walking down the stairs, and some were just loitering in front of the building. The university campus had several buildings, and Bob had parked in front of the library. He guessed that would be the best place to find the yearbook for 1989.

As he ambled to the front door, a group of students rushed by him. He let them pass and then went inside. It smelled musty and dusty, and the air was cool. The hardwood floors were worn, and the white walls had paintings of the university in the earlier decades, as well as the previous librarians, university deans, and previous presidents.

He headed to the librarian's desk and said, "Excuse me, but I'm looking for the old yearbooks?"

The young woman behind the wooden desk glanced up, assessed him to be someone other than a student, and so she straightened her back, pushed her black-framed glasses back on her nose, and said, "I can help you with that. What year are you looking for, sir?"

"The year 1989." He tapped the counter with his fingers as she pulled out the information from the yearbooks and then got up and went to the computer desk. She typed something fast on the keyboard and then said, "You can view it here on the computer. We have digitalized all our previous yearbooks."

"Thank you very much, miss."

She nodded and ambled back to her desk.

Bob sauntered to the other side of the computer table and sat down on an uncomfortable plastic chair.

He looked at the screen. It had the front cover of the yearbook. He grabbed the mouse with his right hand and browsed the book, taking pictures of the student pages and enlarging the image of each male student.

It took him an hour to finish his tedious work. But he had gotten a good list of male students and their images on his phone now. He double-checked if any students were missing from the photos, and yes, there were two male students' images missing. He took a picture of their names, even if he didn't have their photos. He got up and greeted the student behind the counter. "Thank you, miss. I'm all done with the yearbook. Have a nice day."

She nodded and murmured, "And to you too, sir."

As Bob walked out to his rental car, SAC Michael Walton called, "Have you found anything?"

He replied, "I've finished at the library. I got plenty of photos from the yearbook of the male students. I was just about to send them to you."

"I booked you on the next flight leaving in half an hour. I need you to come to the office straight from the airport. We've had a development in this case." His voice sounded urgent.

"Sure. Care to tell me what's going on?" Bob asked as he beeped his car door, opened the door, and sat down.

"No, not yet. I'll be here when you get back," Michael Walton replied.

"Okay. See you in a couple of hours then." Bob hung up and started the car, driving away from the campus area and heading to the airport again. It was a nice day to drive, but his mind was occupied with the recent call.

What's happened? Why is it so urgent to get me back?

Chapter 10

THE YEARBOOK

Agent Bob Morris drove to the airport rental office and left his car there. He went to the ticket counter, got his ticket, and then went to the TSA line, which wasn't that long. He had only his phone and laptop with him, so it didn't take him ages to pass the checkpoint. When he reached his gate, he saw his flight was scheduled to leave in fifteen minutes, and they had already started boarding. He was the last one to get in line and wait for the stewardess to clear him to the plane.

His boss had gotten him a seat by the window near the front of the plane, which was okay. The next seat stayed empty, which was fine with him. More room for his long legs, and he could work during the flight.

He winced as he noticed the dull ache of his injured shoulder. It reminded him of Harley again and the shooting incident where his fellow agents were killed and when they were betrayed by one of their own. He hadn't taken any pain medication with him on the flight, but now he wished he had. The ache distracted his concentration.

When the stewardess came by with the beverage cart, he asked for a drink. "We don't have any alcohol on the flight. We have other beverages like water, soda, coffee, tea, or juices." The stewardess was a nice-looking young woman in her twenties with blonde hair and a blue uniform. She waited for Bob's answer with a wide smile plastered on her face.

"I'll have a cup of coffee, thank you," Bob replied, smiling back at her.

Bob knew the plane's coffee would be abysmal, but it was better than nothing. Besides, the flight from

Boston to Albany wasn't that long, so they would be landing in a couple of hours.

After he received his drink, he opened his computer and downloaded the photos from his cell phone. It was easier to view them there than on the tiny screen of the phone.

He studied the pictures back and forth. Then he noticed something. The last names of the male students: Raven, Dunst, Frost... These three names were familiar to him because they all had their family members kidnapped: Samantha was the daughter of Carl Raven, Tessa was the daughter of Franklin Dunst, and Helene was the daughter of Harlen Frost. All these men were rich and privileged, and all had studied at the university and belonged to the same fraternity when Harley's mother was raped. It seemed even more believable that Harley had done all his crimes to avenge his mother. After going through other images, he found two more familiar names: Jamieson and Fletcher. He didn't have the file of all Harley's victims, but he guessed he would find eight names connected to his mother's crime. It wasn't a coincidence to find five of them in the yearbook. Harley had suspected all these men were responsible, and thus, he wanted to make them hurt by hurting their descendants and taking their money.

Bob stared at the images. Was there any proof that these men had raped Harley's mother? Nothing except that they all belonged to the same fraternity, which was suspected of rape. Also, they were all wealthy. Their parents would have had the means to keep an attorney available if their sons needed assistance.

The plane started the approach to the airport, and Bob had to close his computer for landing. He'd made some progress with the case, even if he had no idea where Harley was now.

Chapter 11

The Meeting

After arriving back at the local FBI headquarters, Bob found his boss, Michael Walton, waiting for him. His tall figure loomed over a conference room table as Bob knocked on the door and opened it.

A stale, thick air faced him when he stepped inside. *These guys must have been sitting here for hours*, he thought. *It smells like old coffee, sweat, and dust.*

Five different faces turned to see who came in in the middle of the meeting.

"Good! You're finally here. We were just recapping the last information that we've got about Harley's escape. And I also shared the images you sent me of

Harley's mother's case." Michael pointed to the wall where the images had been attached to the wall under the heading: Harley's Mother. Harley's case was divided on the other boards in the room. The images of his previous victims were attached to one board.

Bob sat down on an empty seat by the table and quickly revealed the connection between the men in the yearbook and Harley's victims. "Five out of eight is more than a coincidence. And his mother had told the police there were eight men. I think Harley guessed who the guys were based on his mother's description and went after their families," Bob concluded.

"Great! That explains his abduction spree and how he chose his victims. He believed these men owed his mother for raping her." Michael rubbed his hands in front of him.

"I think there might be more to it than that. I think he also might be looking for his biological father. He is the child of the rapist, but he can't know for sure who his father is. Illegitimate or not, he will inherit from his father if he can find out who the guy is. And all the guys and their families in the yearbook are very rich. That's what the police officer said in Boston too. These families had their attorneys ready at the fraternity building when they tried to interview them, and they were not allowed to even have a word with any of the students because the only witness was the rape victim, who had been drinking. Not a very reliable source. The attorneys didn't even want to let their clients' names be attached to a case like that."

Michael's eyes narrowed. "The students would not have attorneys present unless there was something to hide. Someone, or likely more than one student, had contacted their father and asked for help, and the attorneys had shown up."

"Yeah, that was my thought too," Bob replied. He leaned back in the office chair.

"Okay, we have not just fiddled our thumbs here either," Michael started. "Leon here has picked up a trail where Harley went after the gas station. Show him." He turned to Leon, who typed something on his laptop, and soon a pixelated image of a man appeared on the wall screen.

"That's Harley about two hours after the gas station. As you see, he hasn't changed his clothes yet. He's still wearing the guard's uniform."

"Can you see where he is going?" Bob asked, leaning forward. Harley looked the same as he remembered, although his hair was longer.

"It seems he left the getaway car in the mall's parking lot. He didn't lock the doors, so anyone could have taken it from there. We haven't found it. He walked to a mall, and then several mall cameras captured him going to a computer store and coming out."

"What store?" Bob asked, his eyes gleaming with interest.

"A computer store. He was in no hurry." Leon shook his head, bewildered. He was a young man with a pencil-thin black mustache and dark hair. He had rolled his sleeves up to his elbows.

Michael commented, "We don't know what he will look like next. He has always managed to change his appearance."

Leon nodded. "We followed him walking out of the mall and to the parking lot. He picked up another car. We didn't get a license plate, but we have a make and model, and we've informed the mall that if someone reports their car stolen, contact us. We haven't gotten any calls yet. It looked like a woman was heading to that car. It might have been her car."

"Where did he go after that?" Bob asked. Leon was painfully meticulous in his explanation. Bob would rather hear that they knew where Harley went and where to capture him.

"We followed the stolen car to the next traffic light, and then we lost it on the highway. It will take hours to comb through the traffic cameras in the area because he could have turned anywhere or kept driving to the next state," Leon said and closed his computer.

Michael interrupted. "We called you here because we think we got a list of men who could have had a library in 1989 with a nursery and, thus, nursery books. And they had family attorneys." He pointed to the screen, to a short list of names.

Bob quickly compared the names on his list to Harley's previous victims and realized they were the same.

Michael nodded. "Yes, I see you noted that too. Same names as on his victim list. You were right. He is after his mother's rapists."

"So, Harley believes these five at least are responsible for the rape," Michael added. "And based on the case file copies you sent here, we can compare their description to the photos in the yearbook."

Bob nodded. "Let me forward you all the photos from the yearbook, and you can put them on the wall screen." He opened his computer, tapped on the keyboard, and said, "Done."

Michael turned on his computer, and soon the photos from the yearbook were on the screen. His Eastwood-like stoicism had always been impressive, but in a room full of rookie investigators, he was formidable.

Bob had deemed all the other investigators in the room rookies, but he knew they all had useful skills either with following clues or in technical aspects of the case. Some were excellent at profiling the criminals, but he had no idea who in the room was doing that or if they needed to. They had Harley's profile from Dr. Talon, and Bob guessed no one could have made it better because Dr. Talon was also Harley's previous partner in crime, who Harley killed afterward.

The other investigators keenly studied the yearbook photos while Bob re-studied them.

One young guy with metal-framed glasses browsed the copies of the old case in front of him and said, "I think we can identify at least three of the students based on the descriptions Harley's mother gave." He was about the same age as Leon but stockier. "I don't know why the local police didn't pursue this case more vigorously. Charlotte Keller remembered details of the rapists well. Her memory was good, and so were the notes the local police had written."

"I think one of the boys in the fraternity was a son of a judge. They were hesitant to accuse him," Bob added. He had noted that in the yearbook, one photo had the description: *The next generation of judges*. Bob pointed at the photos on the wall and added, "See the last one on the right. That's him. Mark Gunderson, the son of Judge Gunderson then, currently he is Attorney General Gunderson as you well know."

Silence fell in the room. If the judge had covered for his son, then the case would be hard to get to trial. He would not want his family name to be tarnished. But the old case never went to trial. It was still an open case. If it was connected to Harley's crimes, then the old case would tear open all the old wounds and reveal unsolved crimes.

Chapter 12

THE OLD CASE: THE STUDENTS

―――◆○◆―――

Three students, Bob thought. That's a start. If we can confirm that three of them are rapists, that would be helpful. We would have a motive, and we could prove that was Harley's motive. We know five of the fraternity guys were among Harley's victims but identifying them as his mother's rapists would be a start in building the case.

Michael Walton glanced at Bob but then turned his sharp eyes on the young woman who had made the last comment. "Okay, Lara, tell us what you think you know." He leaned back and waited for the female agent to start.

Lara turned her dark-brown eyes to him and replied, "Harley's mother said that one had long, dark hair. Look at this image in the yearbook." She lifted her copy and held out a picture of a young male who had long hair down to his shoulders. The same image was enlarged and projected onto the wall.

No one else in the fraternity that year had a similar haircut. Bob nodded. Lara was right. That was the only one who matched the description.

"Our first contestant is Franklin Dunst," Lara added.

"The father of Tessa Dunst, the victim of Harley's kidnapping case. She was the one he mutilated and dropped off at the hospital," Bob commented.

"Yes, you're right. Harley figured out the same as we have. He just did it earlier than we did," Michael said. He turned back to Lara and asked, "Who is the next one? You said you could identify three out of the possible rapists."

Lara nodded and browsed the papers in front of her and pulled out the image of a ginger-haired young man with lots of freckles. "This is the next one. He's the only one with this hair color. He must also be one of the guys who raped Harley's mother."

Bob and Michael agreed. They had noted the only red-haired one too.

"Helene's father. Harold Penninger. Helene was the youngest of Harley's kidnapping victims," Bob commented, scratching his chin. He remembered well the scared girl who was not violated and had returned to her father in one piece.

What if Harley kidnaps these victims and takes DNA from each one, trying to find a familial match? Bob considered. He didn't say it aloud. He wanted to think back on his cases with Harley first. Could it be possible? He turned his gaze back to Michael. His boss knew him well, and Bob realized Michael had seen something in his eyes as Michael raised his eyebrows as if asking if he had figured something out.

Bob shook his head slowly. He didn't want to say anything yet.

Michael turned his sharp eyes back to Lara and asked, "Who is the third one?"

Lara took out one of the images and said, "This one." It was the image of a tall, skinny man with a group of fellow fraternity members. It was not in the mug shots but was another image the FBI analysts had dug up from somewhere. Bob had not seen it before.

"Why him?" Michael asked.

"Two reasons: Harley's mother said that there was a skinnier and taller one. This one is both. He is a head taller than the other guys standing in this group picture. His name is Arthur McTavish—"

"He was not one of Harley's victims."

"No, he was not. Probably because he does not have any descendants. Harley had no one to kidnap," Lara replied.

"You still think he is one of the rapists?" Michael asked Lara.

She nodded. "Yes, because he is tall and skinny. Exactly as Harley's mother described."

"Anyone can be tall and skinny when they are students. That does not prove anything," Bob commented.

Lara glanced at him curiously and frowned as if she didn't like her conclusions being questioned. "Yes, true, but he has an old mansion with a nursery. His family had old money and old books—books like the nursery rhyme book."

Bob was not convinced, but he didn't need to be. Five of the fraternity members were already among Harley's victims, so this one could be a rapist too. They didn't have to prove he was the rapist. They had to prove that the rape of Harley's mother was Harley's motive because then they could find where he was going next and who his next victim might be. "If he doesn't have descendants, Harley would not get a ransom from him unless he kidnapped someone from his household. Is there anyone he would care about enough to pay a ransom?"

Lara replied, "Yes, he has prize-winning horses. They are worth hundreds of thousands or even millions."

"Check if there have been any recent thefts or accidents at his stable," Michael requested.

Lara tapped her computer and then lifted her eyes and said, "Bingo! One of his horses disappeared, but he had gotten it back. The horse's back leg had been cut, so he could not compete after that incident."

Bob said slowly, "Harley injured the horse when he didn't pay him. He returned the horse after Arthur paid the sum he had requested."

Michael leaned forward and added, "Or he took the horse to show Arthur that he could take any one of them and showed him what he could do to the horse, and if Arthur didn't obey and pay him, Harley would take another horse, a more important and expensive one, and hurt him. Anyhow, Harley got his payment."

"Yes, you're right," Bob agreed. "The two other ones from the fraternity are Crane and Raven. Raven is, of course, Samantha's father. We know Harley tried to get his hands on the Raven fortune and asked Samantha to sign a document giving him all her money. Carl is on the left side of the images on the wall, and Crane is next to him."

"We have five now." Bob faced Michael and asked, "Do you think there are ten rapists?"

"Yes, because of the rhyme. Harley mentions ten in the rhyme," Bob replied and frowned.

Ten! We might never be able to identify all of them, he thought grimly. *We don't have ten different descriptions of the rapists. We only got five now. Could Harley figure out more rapists? We won't know until he goes after them.* He sighed. He glanced at the wall. He had been there for an hour. He glanced at his boss and mouthed, *Can I leave?*

Michael nodded. He knew Bob had had a long day and wanted to go home.

Bob got up and waved at everyone when he opened the door. "See you later."

Chapter 13

BOB

Bob left the meeting with more questions than answers. Where was Harley? Was his motive his mother's rape, or was that a red herring? *It could be either one*, he thought grimly as he ambled outside and inhaled. He remembered how Harley was capable of scheming and acting so well. They would have never found him the last time without Dr. Talon's notes. He had moved to a different city, changed his appearance, and created a completely new person out of thin air.

Bob glanced up at the sky. It was cloudy but not rainy. All his day had gone in Boston, and now he was back in Albany. *It was not a waste of time*, he thought.

I confirmed the old rape case and found some clues that could tie it to Harley, but will it help to find him? He was sure the FBI would not start looking into an old rape case to solve it. Their sole interest was to catch Harley, the escaped kidnapper who also had killed the FBI agents. He realized he was hungry. He had not had much to eat all day. A lot of coffee to drink, but that wouldn't fill his stomach!

He picked up a Tex-Mex takeout on his way in from a local street vendor and then headed back to his apartment. He tossed the takeout on the kitchen table and left his bag on the chair. First, he wanted to take a shower.

While showering, he considered the idea he had got in the meeting. What if Harley was collecting DNA evidence from his victims? They would tell him who he was related to. He had been obsessed with Samantha Raven's family for such a long time, so was it safe to believe that he had taken Samantha's DNA while either living with her or while he had kidnapped her? The fierce way he had gone after Samantha suggested that Harley thought Carl Raven, Samantha's father, was either related to him or involved in Harley's mother's rape.

Bob dressed in a black T-shirt and jeans, and he headed back to the kitchen to eat. He took out his phone and considered calling Samantha. If Harley was listening, he would get a warning that he knew about the DNA. Would it matter?

Instead, he dialed his boss. When he answered, he asked, "Do we have Samantha's or Carl's DNA and also Harley's DNA in evidence?"

Michael sounded surprised, but then he guessed what Bob was thinking and replied, "I can check that. You want to match Harley to the Raven family. Good idea."

"I think Harley might have kidnapped the heirs of these families to find out if their DNA matched his. It was not only about the money. He wanted proof of who he was. Who his father was," Bob explained.

"We might have more DNA samples from the other cases, for example, Tessa Dunst's DNA after she was dropped off at the hospital mutilated," Michael replied. "I don't see how it helps us to find Harley, though."

"I'm not sure either if it does or not," Bob agreed. "It would clarify our standing and what he is after."

"Okay, let me check what we got in evidence, and I'll get back to you," Michael replied and ended the call.

Bob sat down by the kitchen table and started eating his takeout dinner. He grabbed a beer from the refrigerator and sighed. It had been a long day, and still no sign of Harley. *Where is he?*

Chapter 14

Harley

———◆O◆———

Harley had left the area when he took the truck and headed to downtown Albany. He was lucky because no one stopped him, and he managed to get to the city without any problems. His first task was to change his clothes and get a new vehicle. He had money stashed in several accounts, so he could buy a car if he wanted when he got access to his accounts, but without any cards, he couldn't do that.

He looked for a mall and a computer store with internet access. He parked in the parking lot and strolled to the mall. He was wearing a guard's uniform, so he didn't believe anyone would pay attention to him.

The crash had not been on the news, he hoped, and thus, no one was looking for him. *A couple of hours and the situation will be different*, he thought grimly as he surveyed the shops. He found one computer store and went inside. He sent a money transfer to a local bank and then left the store. He surveyed the parking lot. A few more cars had arrived, but it wasn't too busy. He checked out the nearby cars, but none of them were unlocked. Then he saw a woman arriving carrying bags and using the remote to open her door. He quickly approached her from behind, put his hand over his mouth as she started to struggle, and dropped her bags. He pushed her into the backseat. "Stay quiet and give me your keys!" Harley hissed to her.

The woman was so scared that she handed over the keys. "Please, let me go. Don't hurt me," she begged with tears in her eyes.

"Shut up!" Harley told her angrily. He opened the driver's door, sat down, and started the car. The woman whimpered in the backseat, but Harley ignored her. She was nothing to him. He only needed a vehicle to get to the bank, open his vault and get out his new identity cards. He had stored them with a different name, so the FBI didn't find them when he was arrested. He parked a few blocks away from his destination, opened the back door, and before the woman could say anything, he slapped her face. "Stop screaming. I'll let you go here. If you tell anyone anything about me, I will come after you and kill you. I have your address." He pointed at her handbag. He took it and grabbed her purse. "Margo Argyle."

Harley pushed Margo out onto the street and then went back to the driver's side and drove away. *Time to get the IDs*, he thought and parked in the bank's parking lot.

At the bank, he walked inside and looked for a banker who could help him. He needed to get access to his safety-deposit box. He didn't have the key, but he was told his fingerprint would do in case he lost the key.

He spotted a woman wearing a name tag, and he asked her, "Could you help me, please, Marlene? I've lost my key, and I need access to my box."

"Of course, sir." She pointed to the desk and gestured for him to sit down.

"What is your name?" Marlene asked and logged in to her computer.

"Francis Firmdale." That was the false identity Harley had used when he opened the account.

"Thank you, Mr. Firmdale. I'll access your account," Marlene said and added, "Do you have any ID with you?"

"No, see, that's the problem. I was robbed, and they took my wallet with all my cards. I have nothing. I remember when I opened this account that someone told me I could access it with my fingerprints too," Harley explained. "I don't have any money now, and I desperately need some cash. I have some in my box, but that's it. All the cards went with the guy who stole them." Harley shrugged and smiled apologetically.

"I understand. And yes, you're correct. We can check the fingerprints and open the box for you. It'll be a minute. Let me get the manager, and we can double-check the prints before opening the box," Marlene explained and stood up and walked to the back room, and returned soon with the bank manager, Miller.

"I heard you had an unfortunate incident," Miller said as he shook hands with Harley.

Harley smiled. "Yes, it was terrifying."

"It will take a moment to get your prints, and then we'll compare them. If they match, we can open your box for you," Miller explained.

Marlene handed Harley a keypad. He pressed his fingers on the pad and waited for the results. The computer compared the prints and then beeped.

"Green light. All match," Marlene said, smiling.

"Let's go open your box," Miller said. "Marlene, get the additional key. I already have the bank's master key with me."

"Sure," Marlene said and disappeared to get the key while Harley followed Miller to the safety-deposit area. Marlene arrived a few minutes later, holding another key.

"Number thirteen," Harley said and pointed at one of the boxes.

Marlene put her key in the lock, and Miller did the same with the master key. The box locks clicked, and they opened the door. "There you have it, Mr. Firmdale. We'll leave you alone. Let us know when you need to close it," Marlene said. "I have already ordered a new key for you, so you don't have to worry about it."

"Thank you, Marlene." Harley waited for Miller and Marlene to leave before he pulled out the box and placed it on the table. He opened it and grabbed a few stacks of hundred-dollar bills and then a stack of credit cards and driver's licenses with different names. He left some money and a couple of other identities there in case he needed them another time. This was his backup box. He didn't want to deplete it completely.

After he was done, he closed the box and, on his way out, told Marlene that he was ready and that the box was on the table.

"Oh, one more thing." Harley turned and continued, "I had a money transfer sent to this location earlier today. Where do you think I can pick it up?"

"I can check it here," Marlene said and sat down. "Yes, it seems that you have a money transfer. Do you want it all in cash?"

"Yes, please," Harley said, and Marlene counted the money. "Thank you, Marlene." Harley grabbed the cash and put it in his shirt front pocket and closed the button.

Marlene gave him a wide smile. "Thank you for your business, Mr. Firmdale. Have a nice day."

"You too, Marlene," Harley replied, smiling arrogantly. He pushed the bank's door open and inhaled deeply. *What a gorgeous day to be free*, he thought. *Now I have cash, cards, and IDs. I can do what I want.*

Harley left Margo's stolen car in the parking lot and walked away. He remembered there was a car lot nearby. He headed to the used car dealer and bought a five-year-old truck with his credit card. *Owning a car is better than renting; besides, it will take ages for the police to trace this one to me*, he thought. *They don't know Mr. Firmdale and my other identities. Now, I need to get some clothes and change my outlook. Perhaps short hair again*, he thought.

A barber shop near downtown was helpful, and they cut his hair and dyed it black. Next, he headed to his apartment, which Mr. Firmdale owned. He didn't have the key, but the lobby guard was helpful and gave him the key when he provided his new ID.

"Home, sweet home," Harley muttered as he opened his door and stepped inside.

He loved the silence in his apartment. No noises from other cells, no guards telling him what to do and when. The silence was all-encompassing.

He glanced around. Everything was as he had left it. The computers were there, his clothes were in the closet. He ordered some takeout while flipping through and watching different television channels.

He considered changing his appearance more, perhaps new glasses or colored contact lenses, but decided to leave that for the following day.

When the takeout arrived, he gave a generous tip and then headed to the living room. He was the headline news. A crash and an escaped prisoner. He chuckled. *The FBI and the local rescue teams seem to be stepping on each other's toes at the crash site*, he thought as he watched the news clips.

Chapter 15

The List of Next Victims

It was at least an hour before sunset, and Harley had been busy all day getting his new identity and accounts ready for his new life. He had ordered take-out food from the nearby chicken fast-food restaurant because he didn't want to go out now. He preferred the silence of his apartment. It allowed him to think and decide his next moves.

He was sure that the FBI would have found his trail by now and figured out that he had stolen the truck from the gas station. That didn't matter. Even if they followed his trail to the mall, they wouldn't know which identity he was using and where he was staying. His bank accounts were not found during the previous trial, so he was sure the FBI didn't know about his Mr. Firmdale identity and the accounts with that name. He had other accounts and other identities available if he needed to switch.

He frowned as he considered the one man he considered a threat: Bob Morris. He was no longer with the FBI after he had been wounded, but Harley wasn't sure if he had returned to his work. A gunshot wound would take time to heal. Bob knew him when he was chasing Samantha Raven. He had spoken with Bob back then. He'd recognize his voice if they met again. So would Samantha and his mother. In Harley's mind, those three people were dangerous, and they had to be dealt with. He had tried to contact the Ravens, but there had been no answer. He had checked online and found out that Samantha had gotten married while he was in prison. The husband was the real Thomas Austin. Harley chuckled as he remembered he had stolen Thomas's identity and pretended to be him back then when he was dating Samantha. Now she had married a guy name Thomas Austin! And she had a baby.

He took a long hot shower. It was nice when you didn't have to shower with other prisoners. After the shower, he wrapped a towel around himself and went to the living room. He wondered if he should check out the airlines if the Ravens had taken a commercial flight somewhere. He decided he could do that later.

He sat by the computer and typed in the password for his email. He had sent some DNA samples be analyzed to a company that does DNA comparison before he was arrested the last time. He had never had a chance to view the results. He had a sample of Samantha's hair and some from his other victims. He had asked compared to his DNA sample. He wanted to know who his father was. He knew it was one of the students who had raped his mother, but his mother had never cared to find out which one. He wanted to know. Those college kids were all from rich families, and he was entitled to have their fortune.

Harley hummed softly as he viewed the result.

No hits! How was that possible? Who could be his father? He was sure it would be Carl Raven, Samantha's father, but this showed no resemblance to Samantha's DNA, and neither did the others. He had identified five of the rapists, but none of them was his father. He slammed his fist on the computer table and leaned back. All his work was for nothing. His father had to be someone else from the list of the attendants at that party. Who would remember that old event? Only someone who had been there. Carl Raven was dead, but there were still others alive.

Arthur McTavish is also one possibility. My mother said one of the men was skinny and tall. He put a question mark beside his name. He checked on the computer and found out Arthur had an international business. With a bit of hacking, he discovered that Arthur had taken a flight to Asia a week ago and was currently at a conference in Hong Kong. *I can check the other suspects and get back to Arthur if none of the others has my DNA.*

He picked up a pen and paper and wrote a list of his next targets, leaving out Arthur.

Michael Margrove

Charles Donner

Alfred Classer

All these three were there, and they were leaders of the hazing that had happened at the college. He suspected these three could have initiated the rape there too. He based his hunch on his mother's diary. She had mentioned a few other details in the diary that she had not mentioned to the police, or the police had not written them down. Harley had hacked into the local police department's network and checked the police report, and he knew he had more clues than the police.

He typed their names into the computer and found out where they lived. All were living in different cities: Michael was in Los Angeles, Charles was in Boston, and Alfred was here in Albany. He would be the next target because of the local address. He was a wealthy businessman owning several restaurants on the East Coast, but only one restaurant was in Albany. *He did well after college*, Harley thought and wrote down his address.

Then he paused. *I started with families with children because I assumed the one who fathered me would have children. Perhaps my assumption is incorrect. This man might have never got married and never had any children, or not any officially acknowledged ones.*

He went back to his list of potential and assumed rapists. He viewed the three victims he had chosen.

Alfred was a loner. He lived nearby. *I'll visit him first*, Harley decided and underlined his name on the paper. He felt he was correct this time. Perhaps his father was someone who didn't know he existed.

The other two had got married and had children. He decided to leave them for now. He needed to find out if Alfred was his father.

Chapter 16

THE CLUES FROM THE DIARY

Harley pulled out an old butterfly-covered diary from the desk drawer and opened it. The diary was written in neat curvy handwriting. His mothers.

He sighed. Memories of his mother filled his mind. Especially the last moments before he started the fire that killed her and her new husband. He could still see her pleading eyes and hear her cries; he could see her husband next to her, unconscious and bleeding. Harley had been angry because she never told him who his father was, and when he was old enough, he found the diary and read it. He was the result of a rape that was not solved, and his mother had kept that a secret all these years. He was so furious that he could not even look her in the eyes. He had asked her why she never told him, and she had cried and said she didn't want him to suffer or think that he was less loved because of that. He had hit her in the face, and she had fallen to the floor. Her new husband had walked in, and when he saw his wife on the floor, he had charged at Harley, intent on hitting him but failed. Harley had stabbed him with a kitchen knife, and he fell to the floor. He could still see the surprise in his stepfather's eyes before he fell next to his mother. Harley decided it was time to end this charade. He left the gas on and left a burning cigarette on the kitchen table, hoping that it would start a fire. Eventually, it did. The gas explosion had been heard blocks away. Harley had not been nearby.

He returned and played the role of a shocked son when the firemen and law enforcement interviewed him. He could still smell the acrid smoke of the burning house.

He opened his eyes. Enough memories.

His thoughts went to Dr. Theresa Talon, the FBI profiler, who had collaborated with him and turned against her organization, shot many of the agents, and helped him to escape. However, he didn't need a partner, so he'd killed Talon.

Now, he regretted it. He should have shown the diary to her. She might have understood more about his mother and the rapists than he did. He wondered where Dr. Talon had left her notes. He remembered how she had taken notes when she'd interviewed him in prison. That's how their partnership started.

His eyes returned to the open diary. His mother had signed the first page with her name: Charlotte Meghan Keller. He skipped forward to the part where she described the rapists. *One had small hands, like a child's hands or like mine. Smaller than the other ones.*

Harley wrote that down. He had not been able to see the hands in the photos he had gathered online of the possible rapists.

The next clue: *The next one had long limbs. He reminded me of a spider.*

Harley had checked the yearbook and the names of the fraternity of the αβΩ. He couldn't identify who this one was. He considered writing that down but then decided not to because he wasn't especially tall and didn't have spider-like limbs, so it was unlikely that this one was his father.

He continued to the next paragraph: *This guy had a small mole under his chin. His eyes twitched as he looked at me.*

Harley didn't recall being able to see any pictures of the fraternity that would reveal the area under the chin of any of the fraternity members. He wrote this down on his list.

Harley had started with the easiest targets, which had been Raven, Dunst, and Frost, but now he had the results back from the DNA, he knew his guesses had been wrong.

He leaned back. He could tail Alfred first, visit his restaurant, and try to find out if he had small hands or a mole under his chin. His restaurant might have photos of the owner. *That's worth a visit*, he thought. *Perhaps tomorrow after a goodnight's sleep.*

He yawned. It had been an exciting day.

One, two, three, four, five,
Once I caught a girl alive,
Six, seven, eight, nine, ten,
Then I let you go again.
Why did I let you go?
Because you hurt me so.

Chapter 17

THE CALL

Michael called Bob the next morning and woke him up.

"Yeah?" Bob answered the call groggily. He rubbed his eyes while listening to his boss's reply.

Bob glanced at the clock on the table. It was half past eight. Michael was early.

"The DNA is not a match for Raven, Dunst, or any other of his victims, but he certainly did go through the list of fraternity boys. All his previous victims are heirs of the same fraternity members. Your hunch was excellent."

Bob grunted. "Excellent, my ass! We don't have a clue where he is going and who will be his next victim."

Michael chuckled. "Don't be so sure. We checked out the banks he used before his imprisonment, and he had visited one branch downtown. We have him on tape entering and exiting the building after his escape. He didn't use his name, but when we checked the time stamp of the camera recording with the customers, we have his new identity: Francis Firmdale."

That was a surprise. They had gotten lucky finding his trail and his new identity. "Congrats! That's great news!" Bob replied and sat on the edge of the bed.

"My team is currently combing through the residents of the building in Albany. He must have a hiding place with this new identity. It will take time to go through all the records, but we'll find him," Michael said, trying to assure Bob.

"I hope so because if you don't, he'll find his next victim," Bob replied cynically.

"Have you had any other ideas about this case?" Michael asked.

"No, but I believe he is looking for the fraternity boys. He might choose someone close by for his first case. Do you know if any of the fraternity members live nearby?" Bob asked. He had forgotten to check that in the meeting.

"Let me ask, and I'll have someone call you back with that. If we find someone, you suggest we put surveillance on his home and work?" Michael asked.

"Yes, that would be good. Harley is somewhere here in this city, and we don't know where," Bob said. "I think he has more clues about the rapists than we have. He might have heard the story from his mother, or maybe his mother kept a diary that we never got in our hands. Usually, young women kept diaries back then. I'm sure she kept one too. Harley might have it, so if you find his apartment, look for an old diary," Bob said.

"Good, I'll tell my team," Michael replied. "Go get some breakfast and coffee. I'll call you later today." He hung up.

Bob walked slowly to the bathroom, brushed his teeth, and washed his face. He walked to his kitchen, put on his coffee machine, and took out some eggs to cook and two slices of bread to toast. His breakfast was ready in a few minutes, and he put his eggs and the two slices of toast with cheese on the plate and poured a steaming cup of coffee to go with it.

Back to work, he thought. He pulled out the notes from Dr. Talon and reviewed them. *Nothing new here*, he thought. *What to do next?* He couldn't help finding Harley, but perhaps he could figure out who the next victim might be if he was going to go after one of the frat boys that lived locally. He didn't know if there was more than one. *Better wait for the office to call back*. He walked back to the coffee machine to fill his cup again.

The FBI would be lucky if they found his apartment and his mother's diary. That would give them an advantage they had not had before. They would get the inside knowledge of what Harley knew and perhaps also the names of the next victims.

Chapter 18

Updates

Bob got dressed and then considered what to do next. He took out the list of the fraternity members and checked online where each of them was living. He didn't bother to check Harley's previous victims because he already knew where they lived. He wanted to know the other ones. If Harley had not found the man who fathered him, then he would go after someone else next. He knew Harley was still in that area. They had the video of the bank branch and his new identity, so he was still close by. There had to be a reason for it. He suspected it was because Harley's next victim was living in the Albany area. Only one of them lived here: Alfred Classer, a restaurant owner. He didn't have any family. He had not married and had no known children, or that's what his online profile revealed.

Before Bob had any chance to go looking for an address, Michael called back. He sounded excited. "Let's meet at the office. We'll brief everyone on this case."

"Okay, I'll be there in twenty minutes," Bob replied and hung up. He knew they had a hot lead now.

At the local FBI headquarters, the briefing room was full when Bob arrived. He took a seat next to Michael, who nodded at him. Bob viewed the room and noticed the same people were there as last time, except for one new female agent.

Michael started with a brief introduction and then let the new member of the team take the floor. She was a new profiler, Missy Taft, a young brunette wearing heavy glasses and a dark suit. Her updated profile of Harley was, of course, helpful, except Bob thought she had received enormous help from Dr. Theresa Talon's previous profiles. Missy Taft had not interviewed Harley as Theresa Talon had, so there was that. Missy concluded her profile. "I agree with Theresa Talon's previous profile. If Harley had married into the wealthy Raven family, he might have been satisfied for a while, but eventually, Harley would have started to feel inadequate again because the Ravens would still have control of the money, not Harley. Also, I agree that Harley is a sociopath. He is incapable of loving anyone. The people he encounters in his life are just targets, obstacles, or tools to get what he wants." Missy paused and then continued. "However, I think that the recent revelation of the rape of Harley's mother is significant. It's possible that Harley found out about his mother's rape accidentally and got furious because his mother had not told him about it before; thus, he started looking to find out who the possible rapists were. I also believe that Harley might have been behind the arson that killed his mother and her new husband. Harley thought the man was his real father, and if he found out about his true origins, this might have caused a chain reaction:

the arson that killed his mother and her husband, the kidnappings of several young women, and the chase after Samantha Raven." She pointed at the table and the files in front of each agent in the room and added, "You'll find the details of the profile in that file in front of you." Missy glanced around the room and then sat down. Her briefing was done.

Bob nodded. He agreed with all she'd said. He believed Harley could have gone off the rails when he heard about the rape and who was behind it. His chase after these fraternity members proved it.

Michael raised his voice and said, "Let's tell everyone what we've found and what we think will happen next."

He nodded to Leon, who opened his computer and said, "I think I've found where he is staying."

Bob remembered Leon from the last meeting: the young guy with slick dark hair and a thin mustache. He had followed Harley's trail from the gas station.

"We found an apartment building with an apartment leased by Francis Firmdale." He glanced around to make sure everyone caught up with his hint. "The new identity Harley has now." He paused as if he had something even more exciting to tell everyone. "I contacted the lobby guard, and he confirmed that Mr. Firmdale had arrived yesterday and had been in his apartment all night and left it just an hour ago."

An eager murmur echoed in the room after this announcement.

Michael raised his hand and gestured for everyone to calm down. "Yes, we are on to him. We missed him by an hour. Harley, or Mr. Firmdale as he calls himself now, does not know we know where he resides. That's an advantage. Let's get a team out there to watch the building. Leon, would you take Lara with you there? Try to be inconspicuous. Don't sit in an official government vehicle outside his apartment building. He will notice that, and then we'll lose him again."

Leon nodded and glanced at Lara, who gave him a quick smile and a nod.

Michael glanced at Bob and then added, "Bob suggested checking Harley's DNA against his previous victims. There were no hits. If Harley is looking for his father among the fraternity boys, then he has not found the right one yet. We can assume he won't go after the ones he already captured. He had their DNA, and they didn't match. Who will be his next target?"

Bob replied, "Alfred Classer, a local restaurant owner. He has several restaurants, but only one in Albany called The Olives."

Michael raised his eyebrows. "Why him?"

"He is local. Harley is here. Why not take the easiest target? He does not have to travel across the country to find his next victim. He does not know who fathered him, so he'll have to go through the list one by one. I believe Harley will choose Alfred next." He viewed the room and saw approving nods.

"Okay, so we should send a surveillance team out to Alfred Classer's home. We need to check on his business locations too. I think the local one is the most urgent because Harley is in Albany. If Harley goes after Alfred, then we'll have a chance to catch him in action." Michael glanced around the room and continued. "Lara and Leon already have their tasks for today. How about Norman and Grant watch Alfred's house?" When they nodded, Michael turned to Bob and asked, "Would you like to check out Alfred's restaurant?"

Bob knew Michael wanted to give him a chance because he had found out about Alfred and the DNA, so he nodded.

"Yeah, sure. I can do that," Bob agreed. It was better than sitting at home and waiting for updates on the case.

Michael wrapped up the meeting, and everyone went to their desks before heading out or continuing their previous tasks.

Bob lingered behind. "What if I see Harley at the restaurant? I don't have a gun or official FBI status. I'm just a consultant."

"I'll join you. I need to eat too," Michael said. "Let me grab my gun and other stuff. Meet me in front. Okay?"

"Sure," Bob replied. He was puzzled. Michael never went out to chase any criminals. He was the boss. What was going on?

He walked slowly outside and waited there. Michael soon arrived. "Let's take my car. It's over there."

When they sat inside, Bob asked, "Why did you want to go with me?"

"I need to talk to you about your next job with the bureau," Michael replied. "I thought this would be a good time to do that—have a nice lunch and discuss the details."

"Okay, what are the details of the new job?" Bob asked, fearing the worst. *He's going to tell me I can't return to my job.*

"I want you to take a leadership position. You're good at what you do. You've got great investigative skills. You don't have to run and chase these criminals. You could let the younger agents do all that. What do you think?"

Bob was quiet. This was a surprise. He had not expected a promotion.

"I don't know what to say," Bob replied.

"Think about it. We can discuss the details while having lunch," Michael replied.

Chapter 19

At the Restaurant

---◆○◆---

Michael let the valet take his car to park while he walked inside after Bob. They asked for a table by the window. Bob browsed the menu, and when the waitress came to take their order, Michael asked, "Is the owner here today? We have a discreet matter to discuss with him." He casually showed his FBI identification.

The waitress nodded and said, "Yes, he is in the office. I'll go and tell him. It will be a minute."

"Okay, we'll check out the menu and decide what we want for lunch while you do that. Thank you," Michael replied, smiling at the young waitress.

"Do you think Alfred Classer knows why we are here?" Michael asked Bob.

Bob lifted his eyes from the menu and replied, "No, I don't believe so. Even if he has followed the news, I don't think he will connect our visit to Harley's escape. There is no reason why he would worry about Harley coming after him. We have not told the public that he might be going after his previous victims and their families due to a decades-old rape case." Bob returned to browsing the menu.

Michael nodded. "Unless Alfred knows he is guilty of rape, and he recognizes Harley for some reason." He thought for a moment and then shook his head. "No, you're probably right. Alfred has no reason to expect to see Harley unless he had been in touch with Harley's mother or his mother suspected Alfred to be the real father. I don't believe so."

"Harley would have known if his mother had suspected any one of the students as his father. His mother would have told him before he killed her," Bob added.

"Yes, you're right." Michael turned his eyes to the menu and asked, "Have you decided what you want to eat?"

"I'm considering ordering a grilled chicken with salad." Bob pointed at the middle of the menu where the chicken choices were.

"That sounds good. I'll take the same. It saves time in the kitchen, too, if we order the same food." Michael nodded.

***

Harley had also arrived at the restaurant. He was about to walk inside when he saw the two men by the window. He recognized both of them: Bob was the agent who arrested him after Samantha's case, and the other guy was his supervisor, who had been in the news lately. He stopped and returned to the other side of the street to consider his choices and observe the FBI agents.

Harley watched the two men talking and looking at the menu. They seemed to be having lunch, so their reason for being there was just a casual lunch and not to find him. It was bad luck they had chosen the same restaurant Harley had decided to go to. Now he had to wait for them to leave.

Harley didn't believe the FBI was on his trail. He had changed his look and his name. He lived in a different apartment. There was no way in his mind that the FBI could have found him.

While he observed the FBI agents, a third man came to greet them. Harley recognized him as the owner, Alfred Classer. Alfred shook hands with them, but Harley couldn't see if his hands were especially small or if he had a mole under his chin. He would have to get closer to him to check it out. Now was not a good time. Perhaps he could pay a visit to his home...

***

The three men talked about the potential risk that Harley might show up. Michael warned Alfred. "Be careful. If a stranger comes by and asks for you, don't meet him. If someone comes to your home, and you don't know this man, don't let him inside."

Alfred frowned but agreed to do so. Then he asked, "Are you sure this convict is after me?"

"Yes, we are sure," Michael said gravely.

"Why?" Alfred asked, turning his eyes from Michael to Bob. "I haven't done anything with prisons, and I don't know anyone inside the prisons."

Michael sighed. "This is a decades-old case. A rape at a fraternity party over twenty years ago. In March 1989, a young student was raped. Her name was Charlotte Meghan Keller. She is Harley's mother. We believe he is looking for his real father and to avenge his mother."

Alfred paled but didn't comment. He wiped his forehead, and Bob noticed Alfred's hand was shaking severely. *He knows about the rape*, Bob thought.

"Do you remember Charlotte?" Bob asked.

Alfred swallowed and then nodded. "Yes, I remember a young woman with that name and the party."

"Were you one of the guys who raped her?" Michael asked.

"I don't want to answer that question. I don't want to incriminate myself. I should talk to my attorney before answering any questions about any alleged event or crime," Alfred replied. He had gotten his thoughts together, and now his eyes looked cold. "I'm sorry, but if you have any other questions, then please contact my attorney." He got up.

Michael said, "We'll have a team outside your home too. We believe Harley is looking for you."

Alfred nodded but didn't reply. He walked away.

"He is guilty," Bob commented.

Michael replied, "Yes, he remembers the woman and the party. He knew what we were talking about. It was wise of him not to comment on anything without talking to his attorney first."

The waitress took their order, and it didn't take long before they received a steaming hot chicken with rice and a salad. They ate with gusto as the food was excellent. Michael paid for the meal with his credit card, and they left to go back to the office.

They never saw Harley or even suspected that he might have been watching.

Chapter 20

Harley and Alfred

Harley considered his choices. He could leave and try to visit Alfred later, but he didn't know what the two FBI agents had told him. He had suspected they would eventually be on his trail, but not this fast!

Harley didn't believe the FBI knew about his chase after his mother's rapists because that case was ancient in their books. The police had never cared about finding the rapists, even if his mother had given them details of the guys who had raped her. The university had been more concerned about its reputation, and the police had not gotten far with their interviews at the fraternity building because the students had been lawyered up.

Then he had an idea. He could pretend to be an FBI agent, a technical specialist, sent to check out Alfred's security at his home. He quickly assessed his clothes. He had tan slacks and a white short-sleeved shirt. He didn't look like the FBI officer like the two of them, but perhaps the waitress would not pay attention to that. He waited a few minutes more after the FBI agents had left the restaurant and then hurried inside. He looked for the same waitress that had served the agents before. When he saw her, he approached her casually and said, "Hello, my two colleagues were just here." He lowered his voice and added, "I'm also from the FBI. They were here a while ago. They talked with your boss."

The waitress nodded. "Yes, I remember them. You just missed them."

Harley nodded. "Yes, I know that. They forgot to ask something from your boss, so they sent me here instead."

The waitress looked eager to help, so Harley continued. "Could you ask the owner if he would let me check his home security system? I'm the technical specialist. I can do it while he's at work. He does not have to be there."

"Sure. I can go and ask," she said and went to the back office. She returned and said, "Yes, he will let the gate guard know that someone is coming. Just tell the guard who you are, and they will let you in. He won't be home until five p.m."

Harley gave the young waitress a wide smile and thanked her.

After leaving the restaurant, Harley decided to go and pick up his computer from his apartment and some surveillance cameras. He didn't know yet if he would need them, but he better look like he was a technical specialist.

He had walked to the restaurant and left his truck by the apartment building's parking. He walked leisurely back—he had time—before visiting Alfred. He liked being outside because it had been a rare pleasure when he was a convict. He loved the free time, with no one telling him what to do and when. No noises echoing all day and all night from the other cells, no sharing his room with any other convict. He enjoyed the normal sounds of the cars and watching normally dressed people walking by him.

The day was cloudy but warm. He walked slowly, viewing the windows of the bars and the small businesses. However, when he approached his new apartment, he noticed a black sedan lingering near the corner of the street. He stopped and watched. He was sure it was not an unmarked government vehicle. He'd seen plenty of those during his career, but a car lingering near his apartment was suspicious.

Harley withdrew behind the corner and brushed his hair with his hand. *That car looks like it is on the lookout. The FBI doesn't always use government vehicles.* His heart started pounding faster!

How could they know where I live? I changed my identity, and the FBI never knew about this new iden-

tity I had picked up from the bank! The bank account and the safe-deposit box were untouched.

He kept watching as the car idled there. He saw two figures inside. Two agents! He was sure of it. The FBI had found his apartment. He kept watching for a good fifteen minutes, and then, he was sure. No one would just sit and wait there for that long. The driver was smoking and dropped his cigarettes on the roadside. Harley saw three cigarettes on the ground. The car had been there for a while.

He had not noticed it when he left, but he had walked to the restaurant and then waited for the two agents to leave. He had spent two hours this morning on his trip. This car must have arrived after he left the apartment. They had missed him by minutes, he guessed.

Harley quickly backed away and walked in the opposite direction, around the corner, and almost ran to the next corner. His apartment was under surveillance. He couldn't go back. He had to leave his truck there. He cursed silently.

How much did the FBI know? Did they know his identity? Did they accidentally find out where he was staying? Perhaps someone at the building recognized him from the television footage as an escaped convict. It was possible. Even if he had changed his hairstyle, it didn't mean someone wouldn't recognize him.

He slowed down to a normal pace pretending to be out for a stroll.

Another possibility was that Marlene, from the bank. She hadn't behaved as if she had recognized him, but she might have contacted the FBI later that day. Also, the FBI might have caught him on any of the cameras at the bank.

The used car lot was also a possibility. He had paid with a credit card. He now regretted that choice. If the FBI had discovered his identity, they could easily track down his purchases.

He wasn't sure if he could use the Francis Firmdale identity any longer. He had other ones, too, but they were either in the bank or at his apartment. Which one should he try?

He stopped by the window and viewed his reflection. He had short black hair. It wasn't like he had when he escaped. No, it was not likely Marlene had said anything to the feds. He looked different from the guy they showed on television. He had long brown hair when he was transported in that prison van. He could go and check out the front of the bank to see if there were any FBI vehicles loitering in front of it.

He could also try to get into his apartment using the garage or the back door. It was worth a try too.

First, I'll get a rental car, he decided. *It will be faster to move around if I need to.* He checked on his cell phone and found a rent-a-car place downtown and called it. They had several vehicles ready, so he rented one and asked if they could pick him up by Washington Park at the corner of State Street and Washington Avenue. "I'm in a hurry to go to a meeting, so I would appreciate it if someone could bring the car to me," Harley had explained, and of course, the rental office said they could do that. He paid with the credit card, and it seemed there was no problem with it; the FBI had not blocked it or alerted it.

Harley walked to the corner and waited for his car, and in ten minutes, the rental was there. They had brought a second car, so the employee didn't have to walk back.

His new rental was a black sedan. He drove to the bank and around the block to see if any official-looking vehicles were waiting for him. He saw no cars that looked like surveillance vehicles as he slowly drove by and around the corner. He did the route twice. Only parked cars. He didn't notice anyone inside the vehicles parked near the bank.

Harley was right. Michael had forgotten to send a team to the bank. They had not believed that Harley would return there the next day. He parked in the bank's parking lot and stepped out of his car.

The other car he had stolen from Margo was still there. No one had reported it or found it yet.

Harley put on his sunglasses and walked leisurely to the bank and entered. No one was watching.

Inside, he took off his sunglasses and glanced around. He noticed Marlene, walked to her, and smiled when she looked up and saw him. "Could you help me with the safety-deposit box again, Miss Marlene?"

"Yes, of course. You were here yesterday. Mr.?" Marlene replied.

"Firmdale. Francis Firmdale. I had lost my key," Harley explained. "You helped me and ordered the new key, but I haven't got it yet."

"Yes, of course. Let me get our key, and I'll be back soon," she replied and hurried to get the key.

After a few minutes, Harley was back at the safety-deposit box and grabbed a couple of new identities and more cash. He closed the box again, put on his sunglasses, and thanked Marlene on his way out. He exited the bank, headed back to the parking lot, and viewed his surroundings. No suspicious-looking vehicles there. No agents running toward him or his rental car.

Good, Harley thought. *I'm clear*. With new identities in his pocket, he started his rental car and left the bank. He stopped by a shop and bought a new computer and surveillance cameras for Alfred's home visit. After the purchases, he drove to the address where Alfred lived. He saw a vehicle with two people inside it outside by the roadside. He decided to drive to the gate. The guard was waiting for him because Alfred had called them. So, he stopped by the gate and told him his new name, "Jack Frost, the technician for the FBI." He had a fake ID which he showed to the guard who opened the gate. The surveillance car didn't move. They watched Harley and the guard, but because the guard let him inside the gate, they thought he was Alfred's visitor and was on the list.

Chapter 21

At Alfred's Home

Harley didn't hurry when he parked his rental car in front of Alfred's home. He acted as if he was there for a job, checking his clock, picking up his new laptop from the passenger seat and his security cameras which were still in the store bag on the back seat. He didn't glance around or look suspicious. He took his time gathering his equipment and bags. Then Harley walked up to the front door and rang the doorbell.

In a few minutes, the door was opened, and a servant looked at him and asked, "How can I assist you, sir?" She was a young woman with dark hair wearing a simple black dress. She looked at Harley cautiously.

Harley gave the maid a wide smile and replied, "Good afternoon, I'm here to check out your security systems. Your boss, Mr. Classer, approved my visit today. I don't know if he contacted you yet?"

The maid smiled and opened the door wider. "Yes, please come in."

Harley stepped inside to a hall with a high ceiling, polished floors, expensive paintings on the walls, and a wide staircase leading upstairs. The maid closed the door, not knowing whom she had let inside.

***

Michael Walton contacted the two agents who were watching the house. "Any new developments?"

"No, not really. Just one car came by, but the guard let him inside. He seemed to be on the visitor's list," Norman replied. He was the other guy Michael had sent to watch Alfred's house; Grant sat next to him.

"What did he look like? Did you see his face?" Michael asked. He had a sinking feeling.

"No, we didn't actually see his face. His car was a newer model sedan, and the driver had sunglasses and a cap. The cap covered his hair, so I don't know his hair color either. And because of the sunglasses and the cap, I couldn't see his face clearly," Norman replied, slowly straightening in his seat. He sensed something was wrong.

He glanced at his partner who also shook his head and mouthed, "No, I didn't see his face either."

Michael was quiet for a few seconds which felt like ages to Norman.

Because of the long pause in the call, Norman had a sense that they had tanked their assignment. He glanced sideways to his partner who lifted his shoulders and whispered, "What's going on?"

Michael said, "You better check out who that visitor is and what name did he give to the guard. You need to go inside. You can't let people drive in and not know what they look like." He explained it carefully.

He didn't want to reprimand his agents now when they were the only ones on site. For all he knew, the agents might have done correctly. If the visitor was on the guard's list, then he was probably checked out by Alfred Classer. However—

"Call me back after you've checked that last visitor," Michael replied and ended the call. No need to make anyone worried about one visitor. Besides, how would Harley be on the visitor's list? Alfred didn't seem to know him at all.

Next, he called Bob who had gone back home after their lunch at Alfred's restaurant. After the formal greetings, Michael asked, "Do you think Harley could have gotten access to Alfred's home before we visited the restaurant? I mean pretending to be someone else? You know him better than I do."

Bob felt hairs on the back of his neck stand up. The question was what he had not expected from Michael. "Yes, he could have. He has multiple identities. He is an expert pretending to be someone else. He can find any information he needs online. He is a superior hacker." Bob paused and then asked, "Why? What's going on?"

"A visitor came by Alfred Classer's home a while ago. The guard had let him in. My agents didn't see his face. They don't know who he was. They assumed he was someone with Alfred's permission to enter the premises because the guard let him in."

Bob paled. An unknown visitor. "That sounds like Harley. Call your agents! Any servants in the house are in danger!" He grabbed his jacket and rushed outside with his cell phone in his hand. "I'll meet you there." He ran to his car and unlocked it. There is no time to waste if that visitor is Harley, he thought. The only question was why did he go there now? Alfred was not at home. Did Harley plan to stay there and wait for him? Was Harley stalking him? He had no answers to these questions. Harley might be checking out Alfred's home to find out if he has any memorabilia from the time he was at the university and a member of the $\alpha\beta\Omega$ fraternity. Harley could also be looking for a nursery or a library room because of the rhyme book.

That rhyme book had to be part of the answers Harley was looking for. Why else would Harley keep repeating that rhyme? How did the nursery rhyme book end up in the fraternity building? Someone must have brought it with him. Why would someone do that? A memory of home, perhaps? It had to mean something to someone.

Chapter 22
The FBI and Harley

Harley tried to look as professional as he could. He didn't stand too close to the maid and looked the maid directly in the eyes when he said, "I need access to all the rooms in the house. I hope you don't mind?"

The maid replied coyly, "No, please. Do what you need to do. Mr. Classer said you are from the FBI and doing the security system check. The security room is over there on the left." She pointed at the door at the end of the hallway.

"Thanks, I'll start there," Harley said. "I also need to check his office, and on the second floor, I guess, are the bedrooms and the guest rooms? I could install a camera on the second floor to tape all the visitors on that floor."

"The office is on the other side of the hallway. The library is next to it, and yes, upstairs are the bedrooms and bathrooms," the maid explained.

"Okay, I'm all set then. Thanks," Harley said and headed to the security room. He lingered by the doorway, making sure the maid had gone back to wherever she needed to be, and then he snooped around, checking where the different doors led.

Wherever Harley looked, he realized that everything in this house presented old family traditions and money: antique furniture, expensive statues and paintings, valuable carpets, silverware, and porcelain plates and cups on the side table when he peeked inside the dining room. He didn't even know what the purpose of all the rooms were downstairs. Perhaps dining, having parties, and entertaining guests, he guessed. The rooms he was most interested in were the security room, the library, and the office.

He opened the large, heavy wooden door that led to the office. The office had a faint cigar smell. He saw a humidor cabinet next to the large desk. He viewed the desk. A computer. *Easy to hack*, he thought. He browsed the papers on the desk and hunted through the drawers. Nothing interesting to him, he decided. Then he walked to the bookshelf. His eyes immediately latched onto the old tomes on the shelves. *These are first editions*, he thought. I wonder if the book I'm looking for is here too.

Harley leaned closer to see the names, and he took out a few to browse the old tomes with heavy leather binding.

***

The FBI agents arrived at the gate. The guard on duty approached the vehicle and waited until Norman lowered the window. "Good afternoon, gentlemen. What can I do for you?"

Norman said, "Good afternoon. We need to ask about the visitor who came here fifteen minutes ago. Can you please tell me his name?"

The guard was in his forties and was wearing a blue uniform. He checked Norm's FBI identity card and then picked up his logbook. "He is your colleague. Jack Frost, technician for the FBI." He glanced up at the two agents, who had paled. The guard swallowed. "Did I do something wrong?"

"No, not at all. He is not with the FBI," Norman replied, his mouth set in a hard line. They had made an error that could cost them their jobs at the FBI. They had let the criminal they were hunting enter the premises of his next victim.

"I checked his credentials. He had the same ID card as you have!" the guard replied, leaning on the guard's booth window and pointing at Norman's wallet, which was still in his hand.

Norman gave quick orders. "Don't let anyone leave through the gate. We have an escaped prisoner on the premises. I'll call for backup! Stay here and let our colleagues in when they arrive." He called Michael back and let him know what had happened.

Michael replied, "Find him. I'll send backup. I'm on my way, and so is Bob Morris."

After the call, he contacted the sheriff's office and asked for more men to capture the escaped convict whose location they now had. The sheriff replied, "Yes, we will send patrols, and I will contact the local police department too. They will gladly join in the manhunt."

This was the first solid lead they had after the prisoner had escaped the prison transportation car, and it was time to capture him and put him back where he belonged.

Meanwhile, Norman and Grant drove up to the building; they saw a parked car in front of the house.

Grant got out and checked the license plate of Harley's rental car and called the rental company to find out who had rented it: Francis Firmdale—Harley's new alias.

Harley had used his alias because he believed the FBI would not check on his car rental immediately.

"His car is still here. He's not inside," Grant said to Norman, and they both ran to the door. "Should we ring the doorbell?" Grant asked.

Norman replied, "You go in here, I'll go through the back door or kitchen door. Whoever opens the door does not know who Harley is. Don't scare the servant with your gun! I don't want any screams!"

"Okay, I'll be careful," Grant replied and stayed behind while Norman ran to the back of the building, trying to find another door to get in.

He knocked on the kitchen door, and the cook came to open it. She was an elderly, overweight woman with hair tied in a bun on top of her head. She looked puzzled. "Why are you here? Deliveries come here. Guests go to the front door."

Grant nodded and showed her the FBI badge and then put a finger over his lips to ask her to be quiet and motioned to let him in.

***

Inside Alfred's office, Harley heard the doorbell ring in the distance. He stopped and waited for the maid to open the door. He heard a commotion by the door and the maid saying, "Yes, he is here somewhere. I don't know where. I think he started at the security room down the hall."

Harley heard quick footsteps approaching the room where he was no longer.

"He's not here!" Harley heard someone saying. "Where is he?"

"We have to check out the whole building," another voice replied.

Harley considered his choices. He could pretend to be a real technician, but that might turn out badly. He had told Alfred Classer and the maid that he worked for the FBI, and these agents knew that he was not one of them. He could try to hide. It was possible in a house this big... Or he could escape through the window. He assessed the large windows. They had easy latches to open.

He decided to stay still and hide behind the large wooden desk. If the agents were not thorough, they would not see him there. He crouched down and waited. He was quiet as a mouse and breathed in slowly to calm his racing heart.

Harley heard the office door open and someone glancing inside. "He's not here!" someone shouted and closed the door.

"Let's check out the other rooms on this floor and then go upstairs. He might be there," the other agent suggested.

Harley heard steps heading away from the room he was in. He stayed still for a few more minutes. He didn't want to move or make any sound until the agents had gone upstairs. Harley tried to listen, but he didn't know what sounds the stairs made, so he couldn't be sure if the agents were upstairs now or not. He believed he had a few more minutes left before they would come back. He was sure they had called for backup, so he would have to escape somehow. He didn't know yet how.

Harley rose from behind the desk. He walked back to the bookshelves and took out one heavy book. It was a nursery rhyme book. First edition. Published in the late 1900s. Illustrated and collected by the monks, he guessed. He checked out the book and found that some pages were ripped. He viewed the pages and saw that the style of the rhymes was the same as the one he had seen. He had a copy of it. The original was at the police station as evidence.

Years ago, when Harley had started to investigate his mother's rape, he had pretended to be a police officer. He had fake credentials and a uniform from a rent-a-uniform place. He had walked into the police station, and nobody had suspected anything. He knew the case number and had asked to view the police evidence of the case. He had to leave the page behind, but he had taken pictures of both sides.

The rhyme his mother had, was:

One, two, three, four, five,

Once I caught a fish alive.
Six, seven, eight, nine, ten,
Then I let it go again.
Why did you let it go?
Because it bit my finger so.
Which finger did it bite?
This little finger on the right.
One, two, three, four, five,
Once I caught a fish alive.
Six, seven, eight, nine, ten,
Then I let it go again.
Why did you let it go?
Because it bit my finger so.
Which finger did it bite?
This little finger on the right.

Harley turned page after page and then found the place where the page was ripped out. He took out the copy he had with him on his cell phone. He had downloaded it to make sure he would recognize the right book when he saw it. He turned the book toward the light and compared the edge of the page that had been left when a page was ripped off. It was the same book his mother had taken the page from! Or did she take it? What if someone else had given it to his mother without her even knowing it? Harley shook his head. He had more questions now than answers.

One thing was sure. This man, Alfred Keller, was one of the guys who had raped his mother! This book was solid proof Alfred had been present when the rape happened.

Sirens and flashing blue and red lights alerted him. Harley took the book with him, cracked the door open, and glanced around. No one was near the door. He viewed the window. Yes, perhaps that was the way to go. He stepped to the window, opened the latch, and went through. He was out in the garden.

He held the old rhyme book tightly as if it were the most valuable treasure in the world and ran toward the back of the building; he saw multiple officers and their patrol cars.

It was too late.

The FBI agents, the police officers, and the sheriff's men were all waiting for him there.

Harley realized he had nowhere to go.

Time to surrender, he thought. He sighed and stopped. His head stooped. He knew he was done.

Harley kneeled on the ground. He placed the book carefully next to him and lifted his hands in the air so that law enforcement would see he was unarmed. Then he waited for the first officers to come closer, handcuff him, and pull him up and walk him to the nearest patrol car. They pushed him inside the backseat of the patrol car and closed the door behind him.

Harley watched as the law enforcement all gathered around. They congratulated each other even though they were from different branches. He saw Bob and Michael arrive at the scene. They got the reports from the local police and sheriff. They glanced toward the vehicle where Harley was sitting and then continued talking. No one was in a hurry to take Harley back into custody. He had been caught, and they had time to review the arrest.

My time outside the prison was short but useful, Harley thought as he leaned back in the seat. *I know whom to go after the next time I get out!*

Harley had never planned to stay imprisoned. He believed he would find a way to escape, or his attorney would discover a loophole in the case and get him a new hearing.

The book was taken into police custody because it had been in Harley's possession.

The book…

If only I had gotten a little bit more time; if only I could have met Alfred and found out more about him and my mother's rape. He could be my biological father, Harley thought and shook his head. All ifs. The same questions remained unanswered: *Who is my father? Why did my mother have the page of the rhyme book with her? Is it a clue to the person she thought was my father?*

Chapter 23
THE RHYME

Harley sat in the interrogation room, his hands cuffed to the table. He quietly sang the rhyme, changing the words to what he used to sing before his previous arrests:

One, two, three, four, five,
Once I caught a girl alive,
Six, seven, eight, nine, ten,
Then I let you go again.
Why did I let you go?
Because I loved you so.

Bob was behind the window watching him. Michael walked in and stopped next to him. "Do you want to interview him?"

Bob glanced at him wearily. Harley had been part of his professional life for years now, and Michael knew it. He thought about it for a moment and then replied to Michael, "No, not yet. I want to find out about the book he had with him. He stole it from Alfred Classer's office. That book is a part of this case. Besides, it's an old book worth thousands of dollars, and he stole it from Alfred Classer. It's a felony."

"You are still puzzled by the book?" Michael asked.

"Yes, I think it means more than what we know." Bob saw Michael looking at him and added, "The rhyme page was from that book. I know it. Harley knows it. I want to know why the page was in the evidence after the rape of Charlotte Keller and why Alfred Classer had the book in his possession. Why did he keep the book all these years if it was a piece of evidence. It proved that he was at the rape scene. We are missing something. This does not make any sense to me."

Michael nodded. "Yes, I see what you mean. You want to tie up any loose ends in the case."

"Yes, and I think Harley is not the one who has the answers. I need to talk to Alfred Classer again," Bob replied.

"Be careful. He is an important businessman. His family has long traditions on the East Coast. They are rich beyond means. You'll face an army of attorneys if you say that you suspect Alfred Classer of any crime," Michael warned.

"I know that. I just want to see his reaction when I show him the poem and the book together," Bob said and turned to leave the observation room. "You can continue to interview Harley. He might tell you something new. What I would like to know is if he is looking for his father and if that is the reason why he is attacking specific families."

"Okay, I'll talk to him," Michael promised. He shoved his hands in his pockets.

"One more thing. Do we have Alfred's DNA?" Bob asked. "It would be useful to check that against Harley and also run it through the crime databases."

Michael looked at him, trying to read Bob's thoughts. "We can get his DNA from the book, I believe, or from the house because it's still a crime scene."

"Good. Please, do that. I have an unbelievable idea, but if it is true, then Harley is not the only one to be charged with crimes," Bob added and opened the door. "I'll have the copy of the rhyme with me, and I took a picture of the book where the page had been torn. I want to show them to Alfred Classer and see if he wants to talk."

"Let me know what you find out," Michael called after him from the doorway.

Bob just waved and walked briskly away toward the exit. His thoughts were already on Alfred Classer. *Who is this man? What is his connection to the rape case and Harley? Why is this book important? Why did Alfred keep it?*

He had an idea, but it was too ridiculous to be true, but if it was…

Bob pushed the front door open and was outside. He glanced at the parked cars and saw his car at the front of the FBI office building where he had left it after they had arrested Harley. He walked to the car, opened the door, sat inside, and started the car.

Alfred was not at his home, so Bob guessed that he was still at his restaurant, and that's where he was going now. He gripped the wheel with both hands, his knuckles white as he thought about the crimes Harley had committed and what part Alfred Classer may have played in it.

Chapter 24

Alfred's Book

Bob contacted Michael one more time from his car while driving. "Michael?"

"Yes, what is it? Did you forget something?" Michael asked with a patient voice.

"Yes, I did. Could you check on different cases nationwide which have anything to do with a rhyme or a poem left at the crime scene?" Bob said and explained what he had on his mind.

Michael was quiet for a while and then said, "If what you think is true, and if we find out something, then this is a bigger case than we ever expected."

"I know. I'm afraid so too," Bob replied. "I've got to go now. I'm close to the restaurant. I think I'll find Alfred there. Talk to you later," he said and ended the call.

When Bob parked in front of the restaurant, he gave his keys to the valet; he had a plan hatched in his head.

He walked inside and looked around. It was still early for dinner, so only a couple of tables were full. The waitress who had served them earlier was still working. He waited until she glanced at the doorway and met his eyes, and he nodded inconspicuously. It took only a moment for her to wrap up her current task with the other customer and come to the doorway to meet him.

"Do you remember me? I was here earlier for lunch with my colleague," Bob started.

The waitress nodded. "Yes, you're the FBI agent. You talked to my boss."

"Yes, and I need to see your boss again. Could you please go and ask if he has a couple of minutes for me?"

"Sure. Could you wait by the bar? I'll be back as soon as I can," the waitress replied and hurried away.

Bob sat by the bar and asked for a glass of soda water. He didn't want to drink yet. He had a case to wrap up.

The waitress returned from the back office and said, "Mr. Classer can see you soon. He has a phone call to finish, but he will come here to meet you after it's done."

It took about ten minutes before Alfred Classer showed up. "My apologies for the wait," he started and extended his hand.

Bob took his hand and shook it firmly. "No problem, sir, and thank you for meeting me. It was nice to sit for a while. It's been a busy day," Bob replied.

"Please, let's go to my office. It's more private there," Alfred Classer said and gestured toward the back office. He glanced at the bar and noticed Bob was only drinking soda water, so he didn't mention anything about a drink.

Bob followed Alfred to his office and closed the door behind him.

Alfred sat behind a desk on a large leather chair and then leaned forward and asked, "What is going on?"

"You probably have heard, sir, that we captured an escaped convict at your home today," Bob started.

Alfred nodded. "Yes, my maid informed me first that we had dozens of police vehicles outside our home. The sheriff called me later, saying that they had arrested a man. He didn't want to go into details, but he said he was the one the FBI had been looking for."

"Yes, sir. That's all correct. I have some questions for you because of that incident," Bob said.

Alfred's eyes turned suspicious. "I was not even there. I don't know anything about it."

"All true. It's not about that. It's about something the escaped convict had with him when he left your home," Bob replied and pulled out his cell phone. He tapped the gallery of images and found the book, and then showed the image to Alfred Classer.

He glanced at it curiously and jerked backward in his chair. All color disappeared from his face. He swallowed as if he was going to be sick and then blinked his eyes rapidly.

He had not expected to see the image of that book, Bob deducted. *He looks as if he is going to be sick.* "Do you recognize this book?"

Bob got no answer, so he repeated the question. "Can you confirm, sir, if you recognize this book? We have it in our possession because the convict had it in his possession when we arrested him. It's part of the case evidence."

Beads of sweat appeared on Alfred's forehead. He swallowed hard and pulled out a white handkerchief from his pocket. His hands were visibly shaking. He swiped beads of sweat from his forehead. "I need a drink," he said, almost whispering. He swiveled his chair sideways and got up. He looked like he had aged years in a few moments. His steps were heavy, and he was stooping as if the weight of the discussion was heavy on his shoulders.

He went to the side table and poured a glass of whiskey from a crystal decanter and chugged it. He took a deep breath and then exhaled. He seemed to calm down. Then he poured another glass, returned to the desk, and sat down. He had some color back in his face. His eyes were stern when he faced Bob. "Yes, I recognize that book. It belongs to me. He must have taken it from my office. It is not very valuable even though it is old because it's missing pages. If it were intact, then it would be worth thousands, but in its current condition, it is not worth much."

He's trying to downplay the book and its importance, Bob thought. "Okay, so I guess you don't want to add any charges because he stole the book, sir?"

"That's correct." Alfred's eyes were shifting from one corner of the room to the table, and he avoided Bob's eyes when he asked, "When do you think I can have it back?"

"That's not for me to decide. It can be months or years. It's part of the evidence in this case," Bob replied. He opened his cell phone's gallery again and picked out another image; he turned the cell phone so that Alfred could see the image. "Do you recognize this page? It's from your book." He browsed forward, showing another image of the book and where the page had been ripped off. "The page was ripped off here. You can see it's a perfect match. Can you explain this?"

"The convict must have taken one page out of the book. I don't know why," Alfred replied trying to sound convincing.

"This page is part of a decades-old case. A rape case at the fraternity of the $\alpha\beta\Omega$ in Boston. You might remember the case. A young woman named Charlotte Meghan Keller was the victim."

Alfred tried to behave as if he knew nothing about it. "I was at that fraternity, but I don't recall those days so well."

"Ah, right. You might remember this one. She had this page in her possession after the rape." Bob watched the color drain from Alfred's face again and added, "The convict who entered your home was

Charlotte's son. He was the result of the group rape that had happened in the fraternity building. The young woman decided to keep the baby when she found out she was pregnant."

Alfred looked visibly sick. "I-I better not say anything else. If you have anything else to say about this, then please contact my attorney. He is Frederick Frincks at Frincks & Franks."

"Yes, I will do that. Thank you for your time, sir," Bob said and got up. "I think you better brief your attorney about that case and anything else you have in mind. Have a good evening."

Bob saw Alfred grabbing his phone before Bob closed the door behind him. *He's guilty. He knows that we are after him. What has he done besides Charlotte's rape?*

Chapter 25

THE REASON

Bob called Michael when he got back in his car. "Michael?"

"Yes, did you get anything from Alfred Classer?" Michael asked.

"Yes and no. He is guilty. He looked sick when I showed him the image of the book and the page that Charlotte Meghan Keller had in her possession after the rape. He admitted the book was his. He said it is not worth much because pages are missing. He was more interested in getting the book back. He didn't want to answer any more questions after I showed him the rhyme page and asked him to contact his attorney, Frederick Frincks at Frincks & Franks."

"I've got big news for you. Your hunch paid out. When you get back to the office, I'll fill you in," Michael replied.

"See you soon," Bob replied, ending the call and pressing the gas. He was curious. What had Michael found out?

***

He viewed the parking in the front of the FBI office building, but it was full, so he drove around and parked in the parking lot behind the building and used the back door to get inside.

Michael was waiting in his room when Bob walked in. "Let's go. The others are waiting for us in the meeting room. You hit the jackpot with your hunch!" He patted Bob on the back, not revealing what the reason was.

"Let's start," Michael said when they walked into the meeting room. All the members of the team that had been helping in Harley's case were there. Their eager faces turned to him and then to Bob.

Michael sat down at the end of the table and said, "Grant, give us a preview of what you have found out so far."

Grant cleared his throat and said, "We've found ten different cases with rhymes or poems left behind after rapes or murders on the East Coast. They happened in different cities, so we have not connected them before. This time, when Bob asked to look for them, we did so, and we found all of them. There might be more cold cases to fit this profile in other states, but we have not looked for them yet."

Grant waited for the information to sink in and then added, "All the poems or rhymes seem to come from this same book. They are either copies of the book pages or ripped from the original book. At least five cases have original pages from this book we have in custody now." His eyes shined as he said that.

Michael turned to Bob. "You've probably solved dozens of old cases with your hunch. We've sent two agents to grab Alfred Classer to bring him in for questioning. Good work!"

"So, you're telling me that Charlotte Keller did not take the page from the book, but Alfred Classer placed the page from the book on each of his victims. That's why he looked so guilty when I talked with him." Bob sighed. "Great. I would like to know if he is Harley's father or not."

"Yes, he is. His DNA came back as a match," Michael confirmed.

"That means that the criminal tendencies of the father were inherited by the son, Harley," Bob replied.

"It would seem so. Like father like son," Michael added. Then he glanced at him curiously. "Have you thought about what I asked you at lunch? I'd like to announce it now if you permit me."

"Yes, I will come back," Bob said.

"Okay, everyone. Listen, Bob will take over my job here, and he has just agreed to it. I will be the next assistant director," Michael announced.

Everyone clapped; Bob felt uncomfortable getting that much attention. He knew it was the right decision. He was best at investigating, and he would be a good supervisor.

"What are the next steps?" Bob asked.

"We'll interrogate Alfred, and his attorney will try to make a deal. Most likely, he will end up in prison for life, but there he can join his son, Harley. Perhaps, they will get to know each other finally," Michael replied. "Alfred has no way of getting out of this. We have circumstantial evidence, and from the previous unsolved crime scenes, we can match his DNA to the crimes too."

"We already matched his DNA to two of the killings," Grant commented.

"Alfred can't deny his DNA. He must explain how his DNA got to the victims' bodies. There's no way he will get out of this," Michal said.

Bob sighed. Finally, this case was over.

Except, why did Harley sing the rhyme? Was it to remind himself of her mother's rape? Was there another reason?

Chapter 26

Bob and Harley

Bob asked, "I'd like to go visit Harley now."

He looked directly at Michael, who frowned and asked, "Why?"

"I want to tell him about his mother's case and that we have been working on it, and also if he asks, I will tell him about his biological father." He did not mention the rhyme but that was also one of his questions.

Michael nodded. "Alfred Classer should be arriving here soon."

"I'll go to see Harley before he gets here." Bob left the room and headed to the interrogation room where Harley was being held.

He opened the door and stepped inside. "Good evening, Harley. How are you?"

No reply.

Bob sat down at the other side of the table and put on the tape recorder. He knew the whole session would be videotaped too.

Harley watched Bob quietly. His shackled hands rested on the table. His eyes were keen on Bob's face, as if trying to read what Bob had on his mind.

Bob rolled the stiffness out of his shoulders. His old gunshot wound still ached. He had not had time to do any of his physical therapy exercises, and it always cost him in more aches and stiffness. He reminded himself to get back into the routine with physical therapy because he had a new job and many agents relied on him.

Bob locked eyes with Harley and said, "I came here to tell you that we have the rhyme book in custody. We have established that it was the same book from where your mother had gotten the rhyme page." When Harley didn't reply, Bob added, "I know she did not rip the page off the book. It was Alfred Classer."

There was more emotion now in Harley's eyes. Something about the way he watched Bob now made Bob sure that Harley was interested in what he had to say next. "Alfred Classer was one of the guys who raped Charlotte Meghan Keller, your mother. But you already knew it or guessed it. Am I right?"

Harley nodded. This time he answered. "Yes, I had a list of the fraternity boys present that night. I had clues about what the rapists looked like. My mother wrote a diary. She wrote some details in it that were not shared with the local police." He sighed and added, "I was so sure my biological father was Carl Raven, but when I received the DNA test back, it turned out that he was not related to me. What a disappointment. Neither were any of the other ones whose heirs I kidnapped. No relation to me I had to start looking for other fraternity boys to find out who my biological father is."

"Do you want to know who he is?" Bob asked quietly.

"Yes, of course."

"We matched your DNA with Alfred Classer. You're his son."

Harley's hands tightened into fists, and he replied, "Finally!" Then he asked, "Do I look like him? Is he tall? Does he have small hands or a mole under his chin? Those were the details my mother wrote in her diary."

Bob stared at Harley. I guess it's normal to want to know about your parents, he thought. "He's of average height. I don't know about any moles on his body. His hands are of normal size. Those details your mother wrote down might match some other guys at the fraternity, but not Alfred."

"Thank you for telling me," Harley replied. "About the rhyme book," Bob started and tilted his head and asked, "do you want to know what it meant?"

"Sure, why not," Harley replied.

"Alfred Classer seems to have been busy since the university, or maybe even before that. He has raped and killed many women along the East Coast. Always in different cities and locations, so law enforcement has not connected these cases before. Not until now when we got his DNA and matched it to several crime scenes." Bob watched as the realization of what he'd just told Harley sunk in.

"My father is a criminal like me," Harley repeated.

"Yes, you both seem to enjoy abducting women and torturing them, your father even more than you," Bob replied dryly.

Harley inhaled deeply and then exhaled slowly. "I see."

"Why did you sing that rhyme?" Bob asked.

"My mother sang it to me every night when I was a little boy. I thought it was a nice song, but when I read her diary and found out about the real rhyme, I realized she had made up a song to remind her of her rapists. I was a result of a rape, but I guess she wanted me to know about the rhyme." Harley paused and added, "I changed the words after I started chasing the rapists and kidnapping their family members."

Next, Harley chanted, *One, two, three, four, five,*
Once I caught a girl alive,
Six, seven, eight, nine, ten,
Then I let you go again.
Why did I let you go?
Because you hurt me so."

Harley looked at Bob and said, "I captured ten women, all family members of the potential rapists. I wanted them to pay. I let them go when I their families paid the ransom. Some I hurt I admit that. All I did was find out who my father was. I wanted revenge too. My mother never loved me. I know it now. She hated me because I was the result of the rape. I guess she kept me because of her religion or because she wanted to be reminded of what had happened to her. She hurt me so much by not telling me the truth, and that's why I let her die in the fire. I killed her."

Bob had suspected all along that there were more female victims than they had known. Now, he knew. There were ten.

"Well, that was all I wanted to tell you. Alfred Classer will be here soon with his attorney," Bob said and stood up and walked to the door.

"Thank you," Harley said quietly.

Bob nodded, opened the door, and left the room. In the hallway, he saw Alfred Classer arriving with two agents, and his attorney was right behind them.

Alfred Classer stopped by Bob and asked, "Is that convict here? I'd like to see him."

"Are you sure?" Bob asked and added, "He knows you're one of the students who raped his mother."

"Yes, I better apologize." Alfred looked serious.

His attorney said, "No, you cannot say anything to anyone without my presence. We deny all the charges, whatever they are. My client is innocent."

"That might be difficult. His DNA already proves he's the biological father of this convict. He is your heir, Mr. Classer," Bob replied. He pointed to the surveillance room and said, "You can see through the window over there. He won't know you're watching him."

Bob turned to the two agents escorting Classer and said, "Give him a couple of minutes there." The agents nodded and escorted him to the surveillance room. The attorney waited in the hallway.

Alfred Classer walked to the room and stopped by the window. He stared at the person in the other room. Behind the glass, shackled to the table, was his only heir, a notorious kidnapper, Harley. Alfred stood there for a long time and then turned and said, "Let's get on with the charges."

The agents took Alfred away, followed by his attorney.

Bob followed Alfred to the interview room where Grant was ready to start the interrogation. He listened to it for a while. He was about to leave when he heard Grant asking, "Why did you leave the pages of the rhyme book to the scenes?"

Alfred Classer looked at his attorney, who shook his head. "You can't reply to that question. It will incriminate you."

Alfred whispered something to his attorney, who then asked Grant, "He wants to make a deal. If he can spend the rest of his life in prison with his son, he will tell you everything."

Grant said, "I will have to ask if the prosecutor will accept that deal."

Bob said to himself behind the mirror, "Yes, the prosecutor will accept it. They will get all the details and the bodies identified."

Grant left the room for a moment and made two calls: one to Michael informing him about the possible deal and one to the prosecutor's office, who accepted the offer. It would save them money and time if Alfred tells everything.

Bob waited for Grant to return to the interrogation room. When he came back, he said, "The prosecutor said yes, and they will give it to you in writing too.

You will have to tell everything and all the details, otherwise, there's no deal."

Alfred nodded. He checked with his attorney, who commented, "Yes, you can start telling. We have their word."

Alfred leaned back and started his story. "The first one was a young woman at my high school. I don't remember her full name. Her first name was Crystal. She was pretty and flirty. I used to send her copies of the poems in the rhyme book. She said she loved my little notes. I thought she was serious. Then I found out she made fun of me behind my back. She had read all the little poems to her friends, and one morning, when I went to my locker, I found them all taped on the door. Everyone laughed. I was called the poem boy after that. I was so humiliated and angry. I decided to do something about it. I made sure I had an alibi for that evening. I told my parents that I would do my homework in my room. Instead, I climbed out of the window, and stalked Crystal to a remote jogging area, and when no one was around,

I grabbed her and strangled her, and then ripped a page of my rhyme book and stuffed it in her pocket." Alfred smiled when he recalled it. "The police always thought that the poem I had left for her was part of the other poems. Her friends told the police that I had sent her many poems. They never checked that this one was not written on a new paper but was ripped from an old book, ripped like she ripped my heart to pieces. After I had killed her, I went back home. I made sure no one saw me when I climbed up to my room, changed clothes, and then went downstairs and told my parents I had just finished my homework. I stayed with them all evening. We had dinner, and the maid who served us food, saw me at the table too. When Crystal's body was found later that evening, no one suspected me. My parents and our maid gave me an alibi."

Grant asked, "You left the page of the book because she made fun of you. Why did you do that to the others?"

"I only raped or killed the women who did not accept me or who chose someone else over me. I left the page with the bodies because they hurt me, tore my heart apart," Alfred commented. "Like the one who was at the college: Charlotte. She laughed at me in the party. She didn't want to have anything to do with me. I convinced the other students to gang rape her. That was all my idea."

Bob decided he had heard enough. He didn't want to hear the total list of Alfred's kills. He knew now why he had left the pages of the rhyme book with his victims.

Bob walked back to Michael's room. This was going to be his room. He glanced around. Michael had already packed his personal items into boxes. *He is ready to start his new job, and I should be too*, Bob thought. *Tomorrow*, he decided, *I'll be back*!

Also by Bobbie Robins

Samantha Raven series:

I'll Be Your Shadow

I'll Never Let You Go

I'll Be Back

ALSO BY THE AUTHOR

I have several pennames based on genres, and all my books are listed here:

The Starbound Orphans Series: (YA/Sci-Fi)

Starbound Orphans

Starbound Journey

Starbound Hearts

The Galactic Emperor (coming soon)

The Ackley Family Saga:

Lord Ackley's Choice

A Rose So Red

Court of Kisses

A Romance Short story:

Snowbound Strangers

Jaxon Axis -series (Dystopian, Sci-Fi):

Jaxon Axis and the First Crime

Jaxon Axis and the Ice Age

The Lost Tomb -series:

The Lost Tomb

Venomous Dunes

The Lost Oasis of Love

Mummy Returns

The Otis Thorne Thriller series:

Fathers and Sons

Black Dust

The Facility

Death Walks in Washington D.C.

The Ashburn -series

On Death's Door

Finders Keepers

The Kingdom Series (fantasy, romantasy, YA)

Wings of Sea

Wings of War

Wings and Fins

Wings of Shadows

Westerns

The Lady and The Stubborn Rancher

The Lady and The Robber Baron

Bury My Dreams

The Cupid and the Elf -series:

Love Trap

Naughty Elf

Ghost Stories

Cursed Banshee

Don't Go There

The Boy Called Pink

Sci-Fi

The Host

Romantasy

Grimhilde

Titanic Paranormal Novel

Chasing Death

Children's books:

Attack Of the Iguana

Evil Elves

The Underground Cat Academy

Three Ghost Brothers (by A. T. Sorsa)

The Minotaur series:

Minotaur's Muse

Minotaur's Curse

Ariadne's Revenge

Ayla Jones (Dark, Gothic Romance, Paranormal romance, Romantasy)

Donder – the Claus Club series

No Way But Down – Book #1 of the Dragon Prophecy Series

Dragon Unleashed – Book #2 of the Dragon Prophecy Series

The Night Riders

Bloodlines of Revolution – Book #1 of Bloodlines series

Bobbie Robins Contemporary thrillers

Samantha Raven Trilogy:
I'll Be Your Shadow
I'll Never Let You Go
I'll Be Back

Anthologies:

The Tales of Howloween

Find a full list of serial fiction, novels:
https://beacons.ai/arlajonesbooks
Tiktok: @jonesesbooks and @authorarlajones
Facebook: www.facebook.com/authorarlajones
Instagram: https://www.instagram.com/arlajonesbooks

Serial Fiction Sites:

patreon.com/arlajones
ttps://getinkspired.com/en/u/authorarlajones/
ttps://reamstories.com/authorbobbierobins

ttps://reamstories.com/authorarlajones

ttps://reamstories.com/authoraylajones

Milton Keynes UK
Ingram Content Group UK Ltd.
UKHW020037271124
451585UK00012B/895